GHOSTS & GOWNS

A CRAFT AND GHOST COZY MYSTERY

A DRESS DESIGNER COZY MYSTERY SERIES
BOOK 1

LUCINDA RACE

MC TWO PRESS

Editor Blossoming Pages
Cover design by Molly Burton @ cozycoverdesigns.com

Manufactured in the United States of America
First Edition June 2025

Print Edition ISBN 978-1-966424-23-9

E-book ISBN 978-1-966424-22-2

1. Town Hall
2. Lillith Park
3. Grants Gowns
4. Whistlers Inn
5. Twice Loved
6. DB Pharmacy
7. Drakes Bay Bank
8. Police Department
9. Knit or Purl
10. 5 Cents a Dance
11. Polly's Pantry
12. Brewed Bliss
13. Blossoms on the Bay
14. Scoop-a-licious

1

———

I pushed open the wood and glass door to my great-uncle's dress shop. It *thud* against the wall, and I walked into a giant cobweb. I shrieked. Shaking my head, I ran a hand over my hair in case something with eight legs had dropped into it. Setting my tote bag on the wide window ledge, I stepped into the shadow-filled space. "It'll take a miracle to get this place cleaned and ready to open by the first of next month."

I closed the door, shutting out the stiff March wind off the bay of the Atlantic Ocean, praying the heat would warm the place up fast.

Rubbing my chilled hands together, I shoved them into my coat pockets. My fingers grazed my gloves, and I pulled them out and laughed. *That's where they were.*

I hurried to where my mom said the office was. As much as I wanted to keep my hands warm, I patted the wall for a light switch and then the thermostat.

"And action!" Not that I liked the sound of my voice, but the silence was already grating on my nerves. The medium-sized workroom was light-filled, pushing away the late morning shadows.

I spotted a thermostat on the opposite wall near another door. I turned the dial and paused. Relief washed over me when the furnace rumbled to life. A thick layer of dust covered the sewing machines, a large table perfect for cutting fabrics, and a small desk in the corner. More cobwebs clung to the racks storing bolts of fabric. I groaned.

"It's not that bad."

I jumped back to the doorway and scanned the room. "Show yourself right now, or I'll…"

"What? Throw your gloves at me?" The deep voice sounded like it was coming from a poor phone connection.

"I've got a gun and I'm not afraid to use it." Hopefully, whoever was in my shop wouldn't call my bluff.

"Fat good that'll do."

Before my eyes, an older man materialized behind the table. His white-silver hair curled around his face. He sported a tidy mustache and goatee and wore an old-fashioned brocade vest complete with a pocket watch on a gold chain.

I narrowed my eyes. "You look vaguely familiar."

"I should. We're family." He grimaced. "About time someone showed up to help me."

I swallowed hard. "You look like a picture my grand-mother has on her mantel, her brother-in-law, Herman. I went to his funeral."

His voice softened, "Erma has a picture of me?"

"Um. My great-uncle is dead. So, who are you, and what are you doing in my dress shop?" I did my best to keep my voice on an even keel. A river of cold sweat ran down my back. My mouth felt parched like an old, withered sponge.

"Young lady, this is *my* dress shop. I opened this business over fifty years ago and have worked here ever since." The man didn't get up, which was a relief. I kept my hand in my pocket on my pretend gun.

"No. My Uncle Herman owned this shop, and he died here after a tragic accident." I shifted from one foot to the other, wishing I'd kept my cell phone in my pocket instead of my tote bag. I glanced over my shoulder. *Could I escape out the door before the old man catches me, or worse, is he a ghost? I hate when this happens.*

With a snort, he asked, "Who said I died from an accident?"

I sighed. *Dang, he's a ghost.* I'd have to give him some information, and maybe he'd move on. "Five months ago, the police contacted my grandmother. We held the funeral shortly after, but it took time to wrap up my job in New York City before I could move to Drakes Bay."

"Why do you want to move to town if I'm not here?"

"Look. Enough with the questions and no answers. Are you going to leave, or must I call the ghost police and have them escort you out?"

He rubbed his hand over his head. More to himself than to me, he said, "I'm dead. You're the only person who can see me." He looked up, his blue eyes watery. "What's your name?"

Ignoring his comment, I tried to appear taller than five feet five inches. I pulled back my shoulders and thrust my chin up. "Claudia Grant."

"Your father was Alex Grant, and he was married to a sweet girl," he said, shaking his finger. "Don't tell me. I'll remember. Dana. A beautiful girl." He grinned and tapped his temple. "I've got the memory of an elephant." His shoulders sagged. "Am I really dead? I don't feel dead. You're sure that Herman Grant, a dressmaker and all-around good guy, is pushing up daisies?"

The poor man was visibly distraught.

Not making quick moves, I crept around the table. The closer I got, the more transparent the man seemed. I rounded the corner, and my hand flew to my mouth. His feet hovered six inches from the ground!

Stumbling back, my foot hit the rolling stool, shooting it

across the room. *"Ghost."*

He spun around—well, his torso and head spun—his legs stayed in the same space. "Where?"

I pointed a trembling finger in his direction. "You're the ghost." Reminding myself there must be a simple explanation, I hurried from the room, flung the front door open, and gulped air into my lungs. I squeezed my eyes tight and muttered, "It's just your overactive imagination. You don't talk to ghosts; you just see them." I glanced over my shoulder.

The apparition hovered in the center of the main room. I wasn't about to refer to him as Herman. But if he was, why hadn't he crossed over? Isn't that what happened to most people when they passed on?

I clenched and unclenched my hands before turning back to enter the store. I stared him down, and he drifted from the center of the room and perched on the edge of a low-slung chaise lounge, although I could see the entire furniture cushion through his form.

I left the door ajar in case I needed to escape. I crossed my arms over my chest and moved closer to the chaise. "If you're Herman Grant, as you claim, you're dead. I attended your funeral, and there was an open casket. How can you be a ghost and why would you want to haunt the shop?"

"Would you sit down? I can assure you I'm in no position to harm you, nor would I if I still breathed air."

I jerked a small side chair to where I was within two steps of the door and, more importantly, the street.

He nodded. "That's better. Now, we need to establish some facts. The first, my name is Herman Grant. You're Claudia Grant, and we're related. A little-known fact in our family is that we have had a long line of psychics with the ability to talk to spirits that haven't crossed over. It's not a stretch to surmise you've inherited that gift. Especially as you're the first person I've talked to in months."

I wanted to protest that I was a normal person who wanted to create beautiful clothes, not talk to ghosts. When I didn't respond, he continued.

"That must be disconcerting, but tell me, haven't you had a sixth sense about things or seen people others didn't know were in the same room?"

I shifted in my chair. "We don't need to discuss my vivid imagination. What's your story? If you are the ghost of my great-uncle Herman, which is possible by your looks, why are you here? Were you waiting for me to arrive? If that's the case, you can go beyond the veil now. Or whatever happens."

"Claudia, that's a lot of questions. If I'm earthbound, I have unfinished business."

"Is there a gown you need to finish?"

He shook his head. "No, my dear. My death wasn't an accident, and until I know what happened, I'm stuck here. At least now I've got company. You."

I rocked the chair onto its back legs. "Are you saying someone murdered you?"

A sharp rap on the door caused me to drop the chair on all fours and leap to my feet. A tall, thin woman about my age, with auburn hair and hazel eyes, dressed in crisp tan slacks and a pale green cable-knit sweater, stood at the door holding a fluffy cat close to her chest. The cat could be a Himalayan based on its dark face and crystal-blue eyes. The newcomer wasn't wearing a coat; she must be chilled to the bone. I rushed to open the door.

"Hi, I'm Beth Stewart." She bobbed her head to the cat in her arms. "This is Lola."

Herman glided across the room and stretched out his hand to the fur ball. "My Lola. I wondered what happened to her."

Since Beth didn't react when he spoke, I was sure only I heard him, except Lola began to purr and stretched out a paw toward him. "After Herman died, I kept Lola waiting for his family to arrive and reopen the store." She smiled. "And here you are." She handed the cat to me, who promptly wiggled from my arms and strutted through the shop to the back room.

I stretched out my hand. "Claudia Grant. I was Herman's great-niece on my father's side."

She gave it a firm shake. "He said you were an up-and-coming designer and hoped to work with you one day. Of course, that was before the incident."

"Won't you come in? Maybe you could fill me in on the missing puzzle pieces? I was told it was an accident, but the details are sketchy."

She shrugged. "I have time." Closing the door, she gave a low whistle as she took in the dust and cobwebs everywhere. "Wow, you've got your work cut out for you. I can come by later and help with the cleaning."

"That's very nice of you to offer, but I wouldn't want to trouble you."

She cocked a brow. "You have help coming?"

I looked over my shoulder. "No, but as you said, it's a lot of work, and you must have better things to do."

She snapped her fingers. "I have the knitting shop diagonally across the street, Knit or Purl. My dad comes in every day to help. He's a closet knitter. My mom passed away a few years back and it keeps him occupied. It's good for both of us, so I have time."

"Your dad knits?"

"He sure does. He picked it up when Mom was in the hospital. It was something quiet he could do while she rested." She strolled around the space. "Herman would be wringing his hands if he could see the dust bunnies."

Her offer was tempting. "I don't have any supplies."

"That's an easy fix. Polly's Pantry is across and down the street a ways; you'll find everything you need to make this store sparkle. I'll just run home and change clothes. The sooner we get started, the sooner we'll finish."

I wanted to refuse, but talking to someone other than my resident ghost was appealing. "If you can spare some time, I'd love the company. I don't know anyone in town."

Beth's smile was as bright as a lighthouse beacon drawing me in. "You know me now. And I have a feeling we're going to become great friends. Give me a half hour. I'll meet you back here."

"Make it an hour. I'll need to get supplies. What kind of food should I pick up for Lola?"

"I'll bring her travel bag when I return, but I have plenty of food and litter. You're covered for at least a week. You might want to drive over to the Pantry. I'm assuming the refrigerator in Herman's apartment is empty."

I hadn't thought about the upstairs apartment. "Would you, by chance, know where the key is?"

A flash of worry crossed her face. "You haven't been up there yet?"

I frowned. "No. I just arrived. Is there a problem?" I was tired of asking so many questions. "I'll bet it's in a similar condition as down here."

She frowned. "We should look. Herman kept an extra key to the apartment in a cookie tin in the back room."

I gave her a sharp look. How did she know where the extra key was?

"Herman was particular about Lola. If anything ever happened to him, he wanted to make sure I'd take care of her, so he told me where the extra key was as a precaution. Besides, my dad and Herman were great friends."

We crossed the room and entered the work area. She pointed to a tin under the desk. "There it is."

I popped it open. A ring with several colored keys was on top.

"It's the leopard print key."

I laughed for the first time since I entered the shop. "You're kidding."

Herman coughed. "Be nice."

Ignoring him, I said, "Do we go up the back stairs, or is there access inside the shop?"

"He used the inside stairs for storage, so we'll need to go in from outside." She pushed open the back door and knelt to pick up Lola, who was doing her kitty best to evade her.

"I'll carry her."

The staircase was solid. Looking over my shoulder, I was pleased to discover Herman wasn't behind us. Maybe he couldn't come outside. Standing on a broad, covered porch with an incredible view of the bay, I drank in the crisp, salty air. To my right were two rocking chairs, a small table, and a gas grill. "This looks inviting. Maybe after a long day, we could relax with a glass of wine."

Beth grinned. "Count me in, and I'll bring snacks."

"You're on." I slipped the key in the lock, and it turned. The door sprung open, and musty air hit me in the face.

"Herman jerry-rigged the door so it would open easily since he was always carrying supplies upstairs from the shop."

"When was the last time someone was in the apartment?"

Beth placed Lola on the wooden floor. She scampered inside and launched to the window seat, turned around a few times and settled in for a snooze. "Looks like someone's happy to be home."

"Beth, is there something you're not telling me I should know, or do you think I already know?"

"Let's go into the kitchen and have a seat."

She steered me to the right, and my feet froze on the threshold. There was black dust everywhere.

"Dang it. I forgot about this mess."

I whirled around. "Is that mold?"

"Claudia," She placed a comforting hand on my arm. "I'm

sorry to be the one to tell you, but Herman died under mysterious circumstances. The entire apartment was dusted for fingerprints."

I started to take a breath when the enormity of her words hit me. It was just as he had said. "Herman was…?"

Beth took my hand and squeezed. "Yes, his death is considered murder, and they haven't caught the killer."

2

$\mathcal{M}$y knees buckled. Beth slipped her hands under my arms before I hit the floor. "That can't be true. My grandmother was told he hit his head."

Beth helped me to a chair and knelt beside me, rubbing the warmth back into my hands. "I'm sorry I had to be the one to tell you. I thought you knew."

I shook my head. The words wouldn't form. "Do you know what happened and who I can talk to?" The hysteria rose inside of my throat. All I wanted to do was run. "If it's not safe to stay here, I need to find a motel."

She pulled her cell phone from her slacks pocket. "I'll call my dad."

As Beth stepped into the other room, I bit my cheek and swiveled in the chair. The tidy kitchen had a layer of gray dust and black grime on the countertops, cabinet and drawer pulls, and a doorknob that led to an unknown space. I took a slow, deep breath. This was unreal. If Beth couldn't help me, I'd march into the police station, as soon as I located it, and demand answers. Or ask. I wasn't the demanding kind of person.

Herman materialized near the door. "I had forgotten about

the dust." It looked like he was trying to rub the back of his head. With a grimace, if a ghost could, he said, "I'm sorry, Claudia. For this mess and that you weren't told the truth. I'm surprised your grandmother wouldn't have said something about my death being suspicious."

"You remember that now? Why couldn't you have mentioned something when we were chatting downstairs?"

He shrugged. "We were just getting to know each other, and this ghost thing is new to me. I'm not sure what's real or what I've forgotten."

Beth breezed into the kitchen. "Good news. Dad will lock up the knitting shop and head right over. He'll be able to fill in some of the blanks you have."

"Beth, not to be disrespectful, but how can your father help me?"

"Right, you wouldn't know. He's a retired cop. He's got his finger on the pulse of things in Drakes Bay. A lot of his cop buddies bounce stuff off him from time to time."

I stood on shaky legs. "Can you show me around before your dad arrives, and will he be able to tell me if it's safe to stay here?"

"All that and more." She pointed to the door Herman had come through. "That's the back stairs to the shop. Like I said, we'll get that cleaned out tomorrow so you can use it. No sense going outside in the elements if you don't have to."

We walked into the living room. Giving her a grateful smile, I said, "Thank you for being here. This would have been a lot if I had walked into this mess without any reference." I scanned the space.

"That's what friends are for—even new ones." She grinned. "This apartment is one of the best on the street. A few of the shop owners live above them, like me; others rent out the apartments." She pointed out the front window and said, "See the colorful door across the street? That's my place."

With a nod, I said, "Did you paint the door to look like a skein of variegated yarn?"

"Exactly. Someone gets me." Bobbing her head, she grinned again. Did the girl ever frown? "I knew the instant I saw you we were destined to be best friends."

And maybe she had said that too many times. But what did I know about having good friends? Being a geek for sewing had me on the outside of the social scene all through high school unless someone needed help hemming a dress or an alteration, or when I played softball. Design school was the only place I felt accepted, where everyone fought to stand out. Competitive didn't begin to describe that experience.

"You live above your store, that's great. If I decide to stay, we'll be neighbors."

"Come on, I'll give you the rest of the nickel tour." She opened a door near the hallway. "This is the bathroom, and the door straight ahead used to be Herman's office. Once you see it, you might want that for your bedroom instead of using his room."

I felt a chill on my arm as Herman's transparent form went ahead of us and disappeared behind a door to my right.

Beth opened the door—it was a simple room with a chest of drawers, a double bed, nightstands, and a deep green upholstered chair. A small wood valet stood next to the chair. Draped over it was a pinstriped vest and a pair of black pants, as if waiting for someone to put them on. "This was Herman's room. It looks out over Cade Street. I asked him why he wanted to listen to the street noise, but he said he loved the hustle and bustle. Between us, I think he missed Boston even after fifty years."

"I didn't sleep much, so it never bothered me." I glanced at Herman's ghost perched on the windowsill studying his room. "More of the darn black dust in here, too."

I backed out of the room and stood in front of the final door. Beth leaned close. "You're gonna love this room."

"His office?" I turned the doorknob and entered. The corner room was the store's width overlooking the bay and Main Street. Someone decorated it with small floral wallpaper on one wall and pale-yellow paint on the other three. Pale yellow lace curtains draped the back wall framing the expansive ocean view. "I was not expecting this; it's beautiful."

"A few months before Herman died, he mentioned that one day soon, you'd move to town to learn the business. He wanted you to be comfortable, so he converted his office to this. Your grandmother mentioned yellow was your favorite color."

"He told you?"

She nodded. "Herman was a sweetheart, and he hoped you'd take over the shop when he retired."

"Grammie never told me any of this." I perched on the corner of the luxurious bed. Despite the black dust on surfaces in this room, it was perfect, as if I'd decorated it myself. Herman floated into the room, and I looked at his filmy form. "Wherever you are, Uncle Herman, thank you."

"I'm glad you like it, Claudia."

A sharp rap on the door reverberated down the hall, and a male voice called out, "Beth?"

"That'll be my dad." She paused in the doorway. "Are you coming?"

I tipped my head and exhaled. "I need a minute."

"Whenever you're ready. No rush." With a tap on the door casing, she left.

I waited until I heard the murmur of their voices before turning to Herman. "You did this for me?"

"It's not that big of a deal. Your grandmother kept me in the loop on your progress at school and with your internship. When I learned you decided to move to Drakes Bay as my apprentice, I wanted to ensure you were comfortable. You're very talented and will do great things with Grants Gowns."

"I never wanted it like this." Blinking away the tears that

filled my eyes, I said, "Are you here because the murder is unsolved?" We had already discussed the possibility, but I had to ask again.

"Maybe. But I don't want you poking around looking for answers. Leave it to the police."

"They haven't done a good job so far. Your killer is still walking the streets. It's curious: why would someone want to get you out of the way? An unhappy customer?"

"Never." If a ghost could be haughty, my uncle's was. He narrowed his eyes. "Why aren't you afraid of talking to me?"

"Do you want to know the truth? I've been avoiding ghosts my entire life. I'd see them occasionally, but I pretended I didn't. This way, I didn't have to get involved with why they were hanging around, and I never talked to them. It's different this time. You're family." I needed to understand what happened and why. "Now, to discover the reason behind your untimely death. Finding out what happened might prevent me from becoming your apprentice in the afterlife. What can you tell me about the day you died?"

"I don't know what day I became this." He swiped his hand from his feet to his head. "If you could get your hands on my date book, we might find a clue. But it's only to tell the police, understood? I can't impress upon you enough, you're not to take matters into your own hands."

"Why on earth would I want to track down someone who harmed you?" I crossed my fingers behind my back. I'd always wondered what it would be like to channel Nancy Drew. I wasn't going to tell Herman that childhood dream.

"Good." He bobbed his head in the direction of the hall. "Go meet Ethan. He's a good person, and you can trust him and Beth."

I shook my head as I walked down the short hall. Taking advice from a ghost was a new experience for me. The fundamental part of seeing a ghost wasn't my issue—I'd gotten used to that—it was more about conversing with one.

Beth swept the black dust from the counter with a whisk brush in one hand and held a small garbage can in the other. A tall man who was her mirror image except for the salt and pepper strands running through his hair wiped them down with cleaner and a paper towel. I would have known he was Beth's dad if I had seen him on the street.

I crossed the space and stuck out my hand. "Claudia Grant, and you're Mr. Stewart."

Giving my hand a firm up-and-down pump, he said, "Ethan. It's nice to meet you. I'm sorry you walked into all of this. I should have remembered to check the apartment once the police released the scene."

He sounded like a cop. I guessed old habits didn't fade even in retirement. "I see Beth's already hard at work." I half turned toward the living room. "Could we sit a minute? There are so many questions about Herman's death, and I wasn't aware foul play was involved. My grandmother's impression was that he had fallen, hit his head, and passed due to his injuries."

He gestured to the living room. "We should get comfortable."

I sat on the sofa. Lola dropped to the floor from the window seat, hopped into my lap, and purred. Ethan perched on the edge of the recliner next to me. Beth joined us. I looked between them, and a vise tightened around my stomach. I had never seen two people look so grim.

"A few weeks before Herman died, he mentioned—in passing—that a man, Colton Prescott, visited the shop. He said Herman didn't legally own the store, but he'd buy it off him at a fair price. They quarreled, and Herman told him to visit the Registry of Deeds if he needed proof. After that, he didn't see Prescott again. Being an inquisitive fellow, Herman went to the Town Hall. He made a copy of the mortgage discharge page and gave me a copy for safekeeping."

My brow furrowed. "He believed this man was trying to claim the dress shop?"

Ethan clasped his hands together. "I don't think he gave it a serious thought, but he wanted proof in case anyone tried to cause trouble. Of course, records are now computerized, so even if someone had tried to steal the physical information, there would be a digital copy. It was more to reassure Hermanhe was a prudent man."

"That I understand. It must be a family trait to err on the side of caution. Do you know how he was killed?

"Herman was found at the bottom of the stairs in the workroom. It was a blow to the head. The police believe it was staged to look like he had fallen down the stairs. I think that's how the confusion happened. If he had fallen and hit his head, it could have caused death."

Perched on the arm of the sofa, Herman said, "Ask Ethan about the man who said I didn't own the shop."

"Did the police question Prescott about Herman's fall?"

"I'm not sure. I mentioned the meeting and the man's name but never heard they followed up with that lead."

That made no sense. I knew he had an appointment book. "What about his date book or a calendar? I'm sure he kept detailed notes. To be successful in any business, his records had to be organized. Maybe they had another meeting the day Herman died."

"That's it, Claudia. Ethan will know where to look for my book."

I heard the excitement in Herman's voice as I crossed my legs and prayed I appeared casual. "Would you happen to know if he kept one and where?"

Ethan leveled his gaze at me. "He did. It wasn't found either in the shop or in the apartment. To my way of thinking, he hid it on the premises, but I don't know where."

"Why wasn't the dress shop covered with fingerprint dust?"

His eyes widened. "It was. I had it cleaned after they had gathered all the evidence. The shop was a busy place, and there wasn't anything that pointed to his attacker." He gave me a thoughtful look. "They took longer releasing the apartment and I overlooked it. Beth and I'll help you clean, and you can move in tonight."

I bit my lower lip and hesitated. "Is it safe?"

"I've changed the lock to the apartment." He withdrew a ring with a key dangling from it. "This goes to the internal stairs from the shop. I can change the locks on the shop's front and back doors and the exterior apartment door if you'd like. This way, you can be confident you're the only person with keys."

Herman bobbed his head. "Trust Ethan, he was an honest cop."

Was that one of the few comments he felt needed to be said on repeat? I'd have to circle back when I was alone or relatively alone since it appeared my resident ghost would be with me for a while. "Thank you. I'd appreciate that." I placed Lola on the cushion and stood. "If this place is going to be fit to live in, I'd better start cleaning."

Ethan stood, and Beth clapped her hands on her slacks. "I'll change while Dad goes to the hardware store to get the new locks. Who knows, maybe while he's out, he can swing by Brewed Bliss for coffee and a few pastries." She winked, "You're gonna love the shop. The coffee's always fresh and hot, and the sweets," she did a chef's kiss to her fingertips, "divine. Nikki Twing from Pembroke Cove is the baker and there's magic behind that whisk."

I laughed, and it felt good. "I'll go since I need cleaning supplies."

"No need. I checked the pantry cabinet before you came

out, and Herman had quite a stash of cleaners. You've got enough for months."

Ethan asked, "How do you take your coffee, Claudia?"

I pulled some bills out of my pants pocket and passed them to him. "Just cream, please, and here's money for the locks, snacks, and coffee."

"Beth, your tote bag is by the back door with a change of clothes. I'll be back shortly."

Beth said, "I'll go change in the bathroom."

Once alone, I whispered, "Herman, where did you stash your date book?" There was no sense in giving Beth a reason to think I was talking to myself.

He floated into the kitchen and through a narrow door before sticking his head back out. "The pantry is a great place to store things. Pick up the cleaning supplies. There's a small hatch cut into the floor. But move quickly before Beth comes back."

3

———

opened a drawer and withdrew a butter knife. If I had to pry up a floorboard, I wasn't about to break a nail. Moving the bottles of cleaners and endless rolls of paper towels aside, I muttered, "Did you think of using reusable cloths for cleaning?"

Herman's voice was urgent as he said, "We can discuss the merits of paper versus cloth another time. There's a small round tab in the upper right corner of the board under the bottle of window cleaner."

I rolled my eyes, moved the bottle, slipped the knife's tip through the circle, and lifted it. The section of the floor pulled up, revealing a small space between the floor joists. Inside was a dark blue book and a metal cash box. I'd come back to that another time. For now, all I needed was in my hand. I replaced the floor piece, moved the cleaners back into place, and stood, banging my head on a low shelf. "Ouch."

"Let me help you." Beth held out a hand. I stashed the book under my arm, rubbed the back of my head, and got to my feet.

"What's that?" She pointed to the book.

I hated to fib. There wasn't a believable explanation for

19

Herman telling me about his hidey hole. Staying focused on the book, I said, "I was getting the cleaners and saw this wedged against the back of the wall. Do you think it might be Herman's date book?"

"Only one way to find out. Open it." She pulled out two kitchen chairs and gestured for me to sit.

I placed the book on the table and glanced at Herman's ghost hovering beside my elbow. "It's my book, and I'm sure I wrote down details of that horrid man. It's something I'd do."

"Do you know what day Ethan said the man came to the shop?"

Beth tipped her head back and closed her eyes. "A few weeks before Herman died. Maybe look through each page and see if anything leaps out at us."

Herman said, "If you position the book so I can read over your shoulder, I'll fill you in on the specifics of each entry."

I flipped through the pages to the last entry. "Wow, he was meticulous. Look at this; he recorded every minute detail about the bride and her attendants. I should follow up with each of these contacts to confirm they are ready for their special events."

"Even if they're all set, it would extend a good hand to the community."

I skimmed each page, going back in order of date. I paused when I found a page with red ink. "Look at this. Colton Prescott."

"That's it," Herman's transparent finger tapped the page.

"Are there other details?" Beth peered closer.

"It says, deed. Mortgage. Documents and a phone number." I withdrew my phone from my pocket. "I'm going to call it."

She reached over and placed her hand over my phone. "We should run this by Dad first. Just to be cautious."

Beth had a point. I set the phone on the open page. I

wanted to ask Herman about the meeting, so I devised a plan. "Herman was going to all the trouble of documenting his ownership. Why? This dress shop has been here for at least five decades. Suddenly, someone wants to lay claim?"

She pointed to the glass door. "Prime real estate? Taking advantage of an elderly man who, from appearances, was alone in the world? Maybe Colton Prescott thought he could hoodwink Herman into believing his claim and offer him a cash settlement to walk away. Prescott ends up with bay-front property for a bargain price."

Herman crossed his arms over his chest and harrumphed, "Outrageous."

"Have you heard anyone trying to purchase other property in town?"

Her brow wrinkled. "No. So that wouldn't make sense. If it were a developer, they'd have been knocking on everyone's doors for waterfront buildings."

"All right, so no motive there." I turned the date book to the last page and jotted down a few notes. I needed some way to organize my thoughts before Ethan came back. "What about this particular building would make Mr. Prescott want to purchase it?"

Nothing made sense. I pushed back from the table. "I need to clean. It's always been the best way for me to clear my mind. Who knows, we might stumble across another clue."

"I'm the same way." Beth said, "I'll keep sweeping dust if you want to come behind me and wash the surfaces down. We can make quick work on the counters and floors. Maybe even before Dad returns, we'll have one room cleaned."

"Don't forget to set up Lola's litter box, water, and food bowls." Herman floated to the living room. "My baby might be getting hungry or thirsty."

"Once the kitchen is cleaned, I can set up Lola's area." I gave Herman a wink to let him know I wouldn't overlook his beloved cat. "Any idea where she sleeps?"

Beth laughed. "Wherever she wants, it's a cat thing. Lola knows she runs the house and will graciously allow you to wait on her."

With an exaggerated shrug, I said, "Great. I've never had a cat before."

"Oh, Claudia, you don't have a cat," she laughed, "they have you. In time, you'll come to adore her. She has a way about her that slinks around your heart and latches on for life."

Herman grumbled. "At least she held me captive until I died."

"Something else to look forward to." I went to the closet and picked up a roll of paper towels and cleaner. "I'm ready to scrub."

"Then let's do this."

Forty-five minutes later, the kitchen shone. Underneath the fingerprint dust, I was pleased to discover Herman had been fastidious about his home. I beamed almost as brightly as the stainless steel on the stove. "Beth, this is amazing. Marble counters, stainless appliances. I didn't know what to expect. I'll be very comfortable here between the kitchen and my beautiful bedroom."

"Wait until you see the bathroom: an old claw foot tub, pedestal sink, and behind a set of doors is a washer and dryer."

"Fancy."

Footsteps on the exterior stairs drew my attention. "Ethan must be back."

I swung open the door. With a wide smile, I took the bag and to-go coffee tray from him. "Just in time for our first break."

He bobbed his head. "I have locks. When I came up the stairs, I noticed Herman never installed cameras and wondered if you'd want to. You can log in on your cell and monitor things when you're not here, or when you're working late at night and hear a noise outside, you'll be able to look without opening the door. I can do it if you'd like, or I can give you the names of some people around town who do that type of work.""

Beth took the bag from my hand. "Dad's cheaper—promise to buy pizza some night, and he'll do almost anything."

I laughed. "I thought doughnuts would be the best choice?"

"You're quick with a retort. I like it." He chuckled, "Now, there'll be two ganging up on one." He glanced around the kitchen and smiled. "Looks great in here. What's next?"

"The bathroom and Claudia's room. Once you finish the locks, you can dust the living room. If there's time, we'll tackle Herman's room."

"I'm used to leaving dust, not cleaning it up." He took the coffee I handed him.

"Good idea, labeling the cups with our names." I gave one to Beth and then took mine. "We should sit at the table since it's clean." I stole a look at Beth, who gave me a slight nod. She must have guessed I wanted to show Ethan the book.

"Before we do, I swung by the market and picked up a few essentials for your first night—coffee, sugar, cream, oatmeal, juice, bread, and bananas. I wasn't sure what was in the cupboards, and this way, you can eat breakfast. You've got enough on your mind without worrying about a grocery run. I left the bags at the bottom of the stairs."

Before I could speak, he was out the door. "He didn't have to do that."

"That's Dad. Like I said before, he's at loose ends since Mom died, and I'm an only kid. It would mean the world to me if you don't mind letting him help today. I haven't seen him this animated in a long time."

"I thought he worked at your store?"

"He does, but fixing locks, installing security cameras, even picking up groceries, are acts of service ingrained in him for over thirty-five years."

"I'm happy to accept the help. Before you walked into the store, I felt like I had made a huge mistake moving here."

"And now?" Beth's brow arched above one eye.

I looked at the door leading to the outside deck. "If my dad were here, he'd be doing the same things."

The door opened, and Ethan juggled two overflowing brown paper sacks.

I took one and looked inside. "This is more than a few things to get me through breakfast."

"What can I say? I wasn't sure what you liked."

Beth took the other bags. "Take a seat, and I'll put the groceries away."

That was the perfect segue. "Ethan, while you were gone, I found this notebook in the pantry cabinet, jammed against the wall." I slid the book across the smooth wooden table. "It appears this is where Herman kept notes in the last months of his life. Beth and I scanned them and discovered what might be an important clue."

"That's odd. I wonder how the team overlooked it." He looked at the open page and read aloud, "Colton Prescott." He nodded "That confirms one idea."

"Look. There's a phone number. I could call and introduce myself. Mention I found these notes and ask a couple of questions about his business with Herman and then pass that information along to the police investigating his murder. If he's the guilty party, then any information I glean could be helpful."

Ethan shook his head. "No. If he had anything to do with Herman's death, contacting him would put you in his crosshairs. Maybe more so since you're new in town and plan to reopen the dress shop."

"Point taken," I tapped my lips, "and one I hadn't considered. It seems a shame to let the number go to waste."

He took a picture of the page. "It won't. I'll text it to someone I trust at the Drakes Bay PD. They'll follow up on this new information."

A phone rang in the other room. I looked from Ethan to Beth. "Did Herman have a landline?"

Herman said, "I did, and you should answer it. There's no answering machine."

I pushed back from the table and followed the sound. A cordless phone and base were under the side table next to the sofa. "Hello?"

"Who's this?" a gruff voice said.

I blinked hard. "You called me."

"I would like to speak with Miss Grant."

Beth and Ethan were in the room, and he mouthed *the speaker*. I looked at the handset to see if there was a button to put the phone on speaker when Ethan pointed to where it was located. I pressed it.

"Speaking. Who's this?"

"Excellent. I'm Colton Prescott. I was a business associate of Herman Grant. He may have mentioned me."

Ethan made a rolling hand motion as if to tell me to keep him talking. Then, he withdrew his cell phone. I'd follow his request even if I didn't know why, yet.

"How can I help you, Mr. Prescott?"

"Mr. Grant had agreed to sell me the dress shop but didn't get a chance to sign the papers before his accident. Are you the new owner?"

"I am. However, I plan on reopening the shop."

"Why?"

My mouth gaped open as I stared at the phone—what a nosy nelly. "I'm a dress designer and always planned on working with my uncle. He was extremely talented. I want to carry on his legacy."

"Well, in that case, I have some excellent news for you, Miss Grant. The amount I was prepared to offer your uncle? I'll increase it by twenty-five percent for your trouble of moving the business. I'm sure Portland would be a better location for a fancy dress shop than this sleepy little town."

I smacked my hand against my head. This man was an annoying liar and condescending, and this was only a phone call. I couldn't imagine how he'd be in person. "Mr. Prescott, I wasn't aware Uncle Herman was planning to sell the shop. But I'll look through his papers and contact you if you can give me a few days."

"I have a better idea. Let's meet the day after next. Ten in the morning at my home office. I'm on Ocean View Street, number twenty-six. It's a lovely Cape Cod-style home with a fire-engine red front door. You can't miss it. Miss Grant, I'm sure arriving in town and discovering the unanswered questions of your uncle's death has been disturbing. I don't want you to be concerned with negotiating the details."

Before I could agree or decline, he hung up. I sank to the sofa and set the phone in its cradle. Absentmindedly, I scratched Lola's head. "He was rude, arrogant, and condescending all rolled into one brief phone call."

Ethan sat down on the matching loveseat with Beth beside him.

"Did you record his call?"

"I did. It's nothing that can be used as evidence, but I wanted to be able to see if he'd drop any clues during the call. This way, we can replay, dissect, and let the police department know what occurred."

"If nothing else, maybe they can dig into his background before I meet with him."

Beth jumped up. "You can't waltz into his home for that meeting. What if he finds out that you know Herman didn't agree to sell the shop to anyone, let alone him? He might try to force you to sign your name."

"It wouldn't do him any good. My grandmother has inherited the shop and, when it's time, she'll pass it to me."

Herman's hand went through my shoulder as he tried to place his hand on it. "That's not exactly true. I changed my will last year with your grandmother's blessing, and all of this is yours, now."

I knew the color drain from my face, my heart hammered, and I felt faint. "Oh, no. I'm going to inherit everything, aren't I?"

Ethan nodded. "That's correct, and Herman appointed me executor of the estate. He thought it was best since we've been friends for many years, and I live in town. I can help with the details."

I stood on shaky legs and gave Lola one final pet. "I'm sorry. I need to clean something."

4

———

Over the last twenty-four hours, I cleaned the apartment and store until everything gleamed, right down to the windows—inside only, due to the cold temperatures. I reclined on the sofa, waiting for the microwave.

My cell rang. "Hello, Beth. Perfect timing. I just sat down."

"Have you eaten dinner yet?"

"A frozen meal is heating up. You're welcome to join me."

"Forget about that. I'm bringing over lobster scampi, hot bread, and salad. See you in ten minutes and we'll enjoy a quick bite to eat."

My mouth instantly watered. "Sounds great. See you soon."

I hurried into the kitchen and stashed the frozen meal in the fridge and filled Lola's bowls with food and water. It was good that Beth was coming over since I was meeting with Colton Prescott in the morning. It would be an opportune time to run some ideas past her.

My stomach flipped. It still seemed weird to know I owned real estate. After talking with Grammie earlier today, she confirmed I was the sole beneficiary of the property. She wanted me to get settled first before sharing the details of Herman's will.

I turned and jumped, placing a hand over my heart. In front of me was Herman's transparent form. "You can't just pop in and out and scare me like that. You're going to take years off my life."

He snickered. "Company for me."

I grimaced. "A living person would scare me if they crept up on me. Since footsteps don't give you away, you need to clear your throat or something when you float in."

"My apologies, Claudia. I'll give it some thought and get back to you." He rubbed his hands together. "I saw you on the computer today. What have you discovered about Prescott?"

I pulled out a chair and sat so we were human to ghost. "Not much. The Internet provided basic information but nothing about his career or background. He doesn't have a social media presence, just his local address and a phone number."

"Isn't that normal for someone of my generation?"

"I don't think he's your age. I'm guessing he's about fifteen years younger."

"That's unfortunate that he's a different type of ghost." He drummed his fingers on the tabletop, but the transparent tips disappeared into the oak slab.

"No disrespect, but can you stop doing that?" I pressed a hand to my midsection.

He flattened his hand. "Sorry. I didn't realize you were squeamish."

"I've learned all kinds of things since meeting you." I glanced at the clock. "Beth is coming over, and I'd appreciate it if you'd give us space. Maybe you could hang out in the dress shop and mull over the last moments of your life. There has to be a clue about your attacker that you haven't remembered." I hated being indelicate, but it was a fact that he had died.

"I'm trying. The bluntness of your reference to my untimely death could be softened. I have feelings, you know." With that statement, Herman evaporated.

A chill raced over me. "I'm sorry."

The only response was the wind groaning under the eaves. A sharp rap on the glass had me hurrying to the door. Beth wrapped herself in a bright red parka, a white knitted hat with a red pompom on the top, and a matching scarf.

"Dinner has arrived. No need to tip the delivery person." She stepped in, and I closed the door before taking the cardboard box from her mitten-covered hands. Lola trotted into the front hall and greeted her with a loud yowl. "Hello, Lola. Yes, I brought you a treat, too."

"She's had dinner." I carried the box to the kitchen and placed it on the table. Beth shrugged out of her jacket and tossed it on the chair before toeing off her winter boots.

"It's snowing again. But it's not supposed to be much accumulation." She went to the sink and washed her hands. I liked how she was comfortable here, as if we'd been friends for years instead of days.

"This is a nice treat." I stacked a large metal container on the table, a loaf of bread wrapped in foil, and a plastic bowl I assumed was the salad.

"Dad has a buddy at the fish market who gave him a great deal on lobsters. He made enough for the night shift guys at the station and us."

"Is there anything your dad can't do?"

She paused while taking the plates from the cabinet. "Stop worrying about you."

"What are you talking about?" I suddenly lost my appetite. "He said I'd be safe here. Should I leave?"

"You are, and no. He's worried about your meeting with

Colton Prescott tomorrow, which, after we discussed the issue, I've decided I'm going with you."

"I can't let you take more time away from your store to go with me a few streets over. I'll text you as soon as I get back."

She handed me a plate. "Dinner first, and then we'll make a plan. The bottom line is that you're not going alone. It's me or Dad."

I saw Herman materialize through the staircase door. As much as I'd like to say "What now?" I couldn't. The landline rang again. What was it with early evening phone calls? "Hold that thought."

"Hello?"

"Miss Grant, Colton Prescott here."

"Mr. Prescott, what can I do for you?"

"Confirming our meeting for tomorrow at...?" The sentence hung in the air. "Ten. Is that still convenient for you?"

I said, "Yes."

"Excellent. If I don't answer the door, it will be unlocked. Just knock and come in. I might be on a conference call."

"All right. See you in the morning." I hung up the phone.

Herman hovered at my elbow. "Tell Beth you'd like her company. She can wait in the car. At least someone will be close by just in case Prescott gets nasty."

I gave him a slight nod to show that I had heard him before he slipped through the stairwell door. I appreciated that he was giving us space, even if he was eavesdropping. "Beth, that phone call was from Prescott. He's an odd duck and said to come in if he didn't answer the door. I've reconsidered, and I'll take you up on your offer."

"That *is* weird. I'll feel better going with you," and handed me a plate.

I filled it with mouthwatering scampi, a chunk of buttery bread, and a generous scoop of salad. "Please thank Ethan for dinner. I'm not sure how I'll be able to repay his generosity.

This was my first homemade meal in a couple of weeks, after packing up my apartment and moving. Take out was my go-to."

"There's no need. Be a smashing success as a business owner and stick around for a long time." She shoulder-bumped me as we walked into the living room.

I settled on what had quickly become my favorite spot on the sofa, and she sat on the loveseat. Lola meandered in with the most pitiful cry.

With a laugh, Beth tapped the space next to her. "Come here, little lady." Lola hopped up beside her, purring loudly. She broke off a piece of white meat and held it for Lola to nibble.

"Is that lobster?"

"No, cod. I brought some with me. You can keep some treats for her in the freezer. When you need a tiny bit, it's already cooked and keeps her purring."

"That's a great idea. I'll need to pick up some fish from the market."

"Bake it plain, flake it, freeze it in ice cube trays and then store it in little packets of plastic wrap. It's super easy. When you're enjoying something luscious like this, Lola gets her treat, and she'll leave you alone."

"Any other tricks I should know?"

She tipped her head and paused, "I don't think so. If I think of anything, I'll pass them along." She forked a piece of lobster. "How's it going with her? She seems content."

"Being in her home, I'm sure, is comforting, and Herman's things are here so she may feel him around her." Not to mention, I caught her watching his ghost a few times.

"That's true; she followed him everywhere." For several minutes, we both savored our dinner.

"Let's talk about your appointment with Colton Prescott. Dad checked, and the man doesn't have a criminal record."

"The Internet didn't show anything other than he owns

his home, but without social media accounts, it's hard to trace family or friends." I sopped up some of the scampi sauce with a hunk of bread. "Any idea how long he's lived in town?"

"Not really. He keeps to himself. Officially, he's been a part-time resident for about twenty years. It's hard to say when he started living here full-time. No one seems to know much about him."

"A recluse. Interesting." I set my empty plate aside and sank deeper into the downy cushions. "Since our meeting is at ten, I'll leave here at quarter of and sit outside the house for a couple of minutes to see if anyone comes or goes."

A gleam appeared in Beth's eye. "Stakeout. I've never been on one, but it sounds fun."

"We should call it being cautious. Honestly, I've even thought about what I should wear. If I have to make a run for it, I've decided on yoga pants and sneakers, which are easy to move in."

She grinned. "I'll dress the same."

Shaking my head, I said, "You're priceless, but it might be best to wait in the car. If I'm not out in ten minutes, knock on the door. I can't imagine anything he fabricates is worth my time. It will be lies about Herman agreeing to sell him the building."

Beth balanced her empty plate on her knee. "Have you found anything in Herman's papers indicating why Prescott's interested in buying the property?"

"Nothing. All I've come across are copies of the legal documents proving ownership. The place is mortgage-free, taxes are up to date, and Herman's name is on the deed. There's no agreement anywhere, not even an unsigned copy."

"Very curious indeed." She kissed the top of Lola's head and stood. "I'll meet you downstairs at nine-thirty. Dress warmly. The wind is supposed to be wicked cold."

My face scrunched at her Maine slang. "Wicked?"

With a chuckle, she said, "I forgot you're from away. In Maine, we use *wicked* like you would use *very*.

"From away?"

"It means you're not a native, and I hate to be the one to spill the beans, but you have to be three generations deep to be considered a Mainer. But you'll still be one of us, don't worry."

She picked up my plate. "Dad's going to install the cameras when the weather breaks. The wind is"

"Wicked cold?" I quipped, taking the plate from her.

"Look at you, already catching on to the lingo. Stick with me, kid. I'll teach you all you need to know."

I placed the empty plates in the sink as she bundled up. "See you in the morning."

The icy wind howled the moment she opened the door. When it was closed she waved one last time, and I flipped the lock. I hurried to the front windows to watch that she got safely across the street to her building. It's not that a small town in Maine was a mecca for crime like a major city, but it never hurt to be extra careful and there was a killer on the loose.

She dashed across the street as a large white sedan allowed her to cross. It seemed to wait until she was inside her door before it eased down the street. A shiver raced down my back when the car paused in front of my store. My heart hammered in my chest. Would someone get out? I exhaled as the car sped away. I wondered if I should ask Ethan about street-facing cameras—at least until whoever killed Herman was behind bars.

The following day, I dressed in a dark turtleneck, yoga pants, thick wool socks, sneakers with deep treads, and a fisherman's knit sweater under my down coat. I gave Lola a scoop of dry food, refreshed her water, and picked my way down the interior stairs.

During the night, when sleep eluded me, I cleared out the back staircase. I wasn't going to take the chance of falling and breaking something. There was still much to organize, but I wouldn't have to go outside to enter the dress shop. I rubbed my hands together, already looking forward to that task later today.

Herman perched on the worktable. "Are you going out?"

"Yes. Beth will be here in a few minutes. Remember, she's going to Colton Prescott's with me for my meeting." I peered out the back door and clicked the remote starter button for my Jeep.

He appeared to rub his head. "Oh. I forgot. It might be a side effect of being a ghost. But that's a good plan. No sense in confronting him alone." He looked over my outfit. "Are you going hiking? You've got enough layers to keep you warm for days in the Arctic."

"Funny." I finger-combed my long hair. "Beth mentioned it's going to be wicked cold today. Who knows how Mr. Prescott keeps his house? I want to be warm when I tell him he's lying."

"Don't antagonize the man. I might not remember much, but I know he's not to be trusted."

My eye caught Beth striding across the street dressed in the same coat as last night. "Here she comes. Wish me luck, and I'll tell you everything when I get back."

"Claudia, I wish you would leave this to the professionals. I'm worried for your safety."

"That's why Beth's coming with me. Try not to worry, Herman. I'll be back before you know it."

I opened and closed the front door, jiggling the handle to make sure it locked…and there wasn't a bell at the top. That was an easy fix. I'd add it to my growing to-do list. It would be charming, and if I were in the back room, I'd know someone came in.

I walked through the shop. "See you later, Herman."

After satisfied the back entrance locked up tight, I crossed the snow-covered parking lot to where my Jeep idled. Beth rounded the entrance to the alleyway.

"Morning, Beth. Ready to roll?"

She lifted her hand in greeting. "Good morning, Claudia. You're dressed for the outdoors."

"Almost." I flicked up my hood. "Now I am."

Frowning, she asked, "Don't you have a hat?"

"I did, but apparently, I left it in the city. I'll be fine."

"Do you want me to drive? We can head across the street and grab my SUV." She pulled keys from her pocket.

"No, thanks. It'll help me learn my way around town."

"Nice wheels," Beth whistled in appreciation. "Perfect for our winter weather, too."

We climbed in. I set my GPS to Mr. Prescott's address. We'd arrive in four minutes, based on current traffic. I eased onto Cade Street and turned right. "The town is quaint. How's your business?"

"During the winter, it's steady with knitters, but it gets hectic in the summer with tourists. They like to purchase specialty wools for winter projects. I was thinking, you might consider keeping the ready-wear section stocked with sundresses and party frocks. Herman used to do that, and it was a steady business that enhanced sales for his wedding gowns and other custom work. I'm sure he kept records of his inventory."

"Thanks. That's a great tip." And, as a bonus, I could ask for his advice, too.

"We've got some time. Do you want a quick tour of downtown?"

"Great." I glanced in my rearview mirror and no one was behind me, so I slowed down.

"Turn left after the park."

I did as she suggested. "It's a big space. What's it called?'

"Lilith Park. It was renamed about fifty years ago. I'm fuzzy on the why, but it was better than what we used to call it."

"Which was?"

She laughed. "The park. We have all kinds of town picnics there; the Christmas tree and Menorah are set up in the center. There's even a gazebo for weddings." She pointed for me to take a right. "Up ahead is Ocean View. Prescott's house will be at the opposite end."

A dark, late-model pickup truck roared past us as I drove cautiously down the street. "They're in a hurry."

I slowed when the GPS indicated I had arrived at my destination. Large evergreen shrubs lined the street, obscuring the view to the house, except for a wide walkway that led to the steps. A white sedan was in the driveway. It resembled the car I saw last night cruising down Main Street. The weathered Cape Cod-style home with a bright red door and black shutters nestled among the maple trees caught my eye. Large evergreen bushes flanked the door. Aside from the walkway from the street, the house was private. "This must be the place." I gripped the steering wheel tighter, noticing my hands had a slight tremble. "It looks deserted."

"He's a loner."

I parked with a clear view of the front door, turned off the Jeep, and left the keys in the ignition. "If you get chilly, turn it back on. I won't be long."

She studied the house. "Are you sure you don't want me to come with you?"

"I'll be fine." Could I be confronting a cold-blooded killer? The thought chilled my blood more than the winter air seeping into the vehicle. "I need a minute or two."

"Take all the time you need. Mr. Prescott isn't going

anywhere. Besides, he asked to see you, so making him cool his heels might be good."

Ten minutes or more later I opened the Jeep door and hopped out. Working on my confidence, I pulled back my shoulders and strode up the walk. A circular, black, wrought iron door knocker positioned mid-door begged to be used. I rapped three times. The door groaned and eased open. This was just like every horror movie I had never watched.

5

———

"**M**r. Prescott? It's Claudia Grant. May I come in?"

I pushed the door wide and stepped in. The entrance was sparse, with a side table, lamp, and a wall mirror. The house was much colder than I expected. He must like it that way. I took another few steps. "Mr. Prescott?"

The hair on the back of my neck stood at attention. The reasonable voice in my head was urging me to leave, but I ignored it and looked to the left. The living room. Neat as a pin. To my right was another doorway, his office perhaps. "Mr. Prescott?" I hovered in the doorway. "It's Claudia Grant. Are you here? We had a meeting at ten."

I scanned the room, and my heart stuttered. From the far side of the desk, a black loafer was visible, and it was on a foot! I crept around the side and jumped back, knocking a stack of folders from the corner of the desk onto the floor. My hand flew to my mouth. I screamed, whirled around, and raced for the door, crashing into a side table with a lamp only slowing when I reached the top step. Waving my arms, I called, "Beth! Come quick. He's dead!

The Jeep door slammed, and she raced up the walk, skidding to a stop in the entrance. Her mouth gaped open in shock. "What's happened?"

"There's a dead man behind a desk. It must be Colton Prescott." I grabbed her hand and dragged her across the hall into the office. "It's his house. It has to be him, right?"

Beth scanned the room, and we moved cautiously toward the desk. "Did you touch anything?"

"I knocked some stuff over, like the table and folders." My steps halted as we reached the corner of the desk. Clutching her arm, I pointed to the man prone on the floor. For the first time, I noticed the pool of blood under his upper body and neck. "Look."

"Mr. Prescott?" her voice shook. "We should check for a pulse."

I swallowed a lump and croaked, "I'll feel his wrist." Being careful to avoid the circle of blood, I bent over him. When my fingers grazed his ice-cold hand, I stepped back. I shuddered. "We need to call the police."

A door banged somewhere in the house. Beth and I froze in place. My worst nightmare was coming true—we weren't alone.

Bobbing my head toward the sound, I whispered, "We should investigate."

She shook her head. "No."

I pointed to the hall and mouthed, *"Stay here."* I stepped over the body, and the toe of my sneaker connected with something that skidded under an upholstered chair. Kneeling, I felt around, and my fingers wrapped around a hard, round cylinder. I slid it out. A ringing began in my ears. It was a gun, and now my fingerprints were on it.

"Freeze! You, on the floor. Drop the weapon, hands up!"

I glanced at Beth, who had her hands in the air. I pivoted on the balls of my feet.

Hovering in the archway was a police officer, gun drawn and trained on me.

I did as the officer said, letting the weapon slip from my fingertips and thrust my arms over my head. "Thank goodness you're here. It's not my gun."

"Get up. Slowly."

Beth said, "Amos, relax. That's my friend Claudia Grant. We found him like this; we didn't shoot him."

The cop lowered his gun but kept it at his side. Did he think I was still a threat?

"What happened?" He scanned the scene, his gaze fixed on the top of the man's head and slid to me.

I lowered my arms in triple slow motion. In a rush I said, "I had an appointment with Colton Prescott at ten. Beth came with me. When I got to the front door, it was ajar. I knocked, it eased open, and when he didn't answer, I came in. The house was cold, and I called out for Mr. Prescott, but he didn't respond."

Another police officer entered the room but didn't identify himself. What was it with these cops? Didn't they have to? He took in the scene. "Do you always enter a home without being invited in?" The blue-eyed cop holstered his weapon, but I didn't like the unflinching stare. He set my teeth on edge even if he was smoking hot.

"We had an appointment, but he said he might be on a call and to come inside. I thought it was odd when I discovered the door ajar. I called out to him, and when he didn't answer, I entered. How was I to know if he had fallen or needed assistance?" That answer sounded convoluted, but it was true. Even if curiosity propelled me into the house, I'd never ignore someone in distress. My natural inclination was to help.

Beth tipped her head. "How did you know to come? We haven't called 9-1-1 yet."

Officer Amos said, "I received a tip of a reported gunshot at this address."

My brow furrowed. "Beth?"

Her voice had an edge as she said, "Amos, I'm calling my dad." She gave me a comforting nod, strode from the room, and nodded to the other police officer who stared at me.

Officer Amos pushed past me and knelt beside Mr. Prescott. "Did you touch the body?"

"Yes, sir. Beth and I thought we should check for a pulse. My fingertips grazed his wrist. It was cold and stiff, so I knew he was dead."

He looked over his shoulder to the second cop. "Officer Jacobs, call in for transport and the crime scene team." He stepped around the desk and pointed to the revolver on the floor. "Is that yours?"

"No, sir. We heard a door bang at the back of the house. I was going to investigate and kicked something under the chair. I pulled it out, and you walked in."

His stare was unflinching. "You may have contaminated critical evidence."

I stuffed my hands in my coat pocket. "That wasn't my intention. I've never stumbled onto a dead body or a crime scene."

His brow arched. "You seem to be a mite defensive."

I didn't like the hostile tone in his voice. "Wouldn't you be if you were in my shoes?" I smacked my hand to my forehead and, muttering more to myself, I said, "I've lived in this town for three days. So far, I discovered my uncle's death is a suspected murder; my store looked like an abandoned haunted house with cobwebs everywhere. My apartment had a layer of fingerprint dust, and some man demanded I meet him here. Now he's dead. What's next?"

He huffed, "Ms. Grant?" Officer Amos gestured toward the front entrance, where Beth was on the phone. "I have a few questions."

I looked at poor Mr. Prescott, his arms at his sides, his hand clutching a chain. This was one mental image I'd never forget. "Does blood normally get that dark?"

"When it's exposed to air, it does." He pointed to the stairs. "Have a seat, and don't move."

I did as he demanded, clasping my hands under my sweater. It was cold in this house.

Beth put her phone in her coat pocket.

"What did your dad say?"

She gave me a reassuring nod. "He's on his way."

"That's a relief."

"Now," Amos stood, feet shoulder-width apart, hands resting on his gun holster, "tell me again what happened. Starting with the bit you just moved to town."

"Claudia's Herman Grant's great niece. She moved here three days ago to reopen the dress shop."

He cocked a brow. "Three days? This must be a record. You're already involved with a homicide, Ms. Grant. You're either a terrible criminal or a very unlucky woman."

"My middle name has never been luck, except for meeting Beth and Ethan on my first day in town. They helped me clean the apartment. I had no idea my uncle had been murdered or that the killer remains at large." I gave him a harsh look. "Since Mr. Prescott called me on my first night in town and demanded I see him, stating my uncle had agreed to sell him the dress shop building, I'd say the two deaths are related and not by me as the killer."

His brow arched. "Revenge is a strong motivator."

"Amos, you can't be serious. I'll vouch for Claudia. She's no more a murderer than I am. Ask Dad if you don't take my word for it."

"Do you have proof Prescott called you two nights ago?"

I sat up straighter. "Yes. Ethan and Beth were in my apartment when he called, and Ethan recorded it so I could listen to the conversation again. I dealt with so many shocks that day, I was overwhelmed."

He rubbed his hand over his chin. "I don't condone recording phone conversations, but in this case, it might keep you out of jail unless someone comes forward and puts you at this house before you arrived with Beth. Did you speak to Mr. Prescott any other time?"

I nodded. "He confirmed our meeting yesterday."

The officer asked, "Did you record that conversation, too?"

"No." Now, I wished I had to prove I wasn't lying.

Officer Jacobs came inside and closed the door. "The team will arrive in a few minutes, Officer Branson."

"Good. The ladies were filling me in on a few details. Of course, we'll bring them to the station and chat on the record and get their fingerprints."

I didn't like the tone or context of his comments. "Officers, I can promise you everything is exactly as I said. Mr. Prescott insisted that he had an agreement with my uncle and was prepared to sweeten the deal to get me to sell the building. Before you ask, I have no idea why he wanted to buy the property. Still, from my conversation with Ethan, the executor of my uncle's estate, Herman didn't intend to relinquish ownership. He planned for me to take over the business when he retired." I dropped my chin. Exhaustion crashed over me like a rogue wave from the bay.

"Officer Branson, I have a question for our suspect."

Amos waved his hand, "By all means, ask."

"Where were you when your uncle died?" Officer Jacobs looked down at me, his eyes filled with suspicion.

"Until two weeks ago, I worked in a design house as a junior apprentice in New York City, and yes, someone can vouch for me. I had four roommates and used public transportation, so there are records that my transit pass was used daily, and my co-workers will confirm I was at work every day. I have an alibi, and for your information, I didn't even know Herman had been murdered until Ethan told me." I figured it was easier to be transparent before they started asking all those questions. I had watched enough cop shows to know that, at this point, I was the primary suspect.

Putting her hand on my shoulder, Beth said, "Back off, Eddie."

"Beth, don't interfere in an ongoing investigation."

She popped her hands on her hips. "Don't tell me what to do. We're not kids anymore. You can't boss me or Claudia around."

"No. I'm a police officer charged with upholding and defending the law. If you think I'll look the other way because this woman is your new friend, you're wrong. Now step aside and let me do my job."

A tentative knock on the door made us look. Officer Jacobson put his hand out to stop me from getting up. "Stay put."

I rounded my shoulders, wishing I could disappear. Maybe if I closed my eyes, this would be a bad dream, and I'd wake up in my own bed. Instead, he opened the door. Three women around my age stood on the porch.

"Eddie. Is everything alright? We noticed the police cruisers." One tried to look around him. She saw me and Beth, and her eyes widened. "Could we come inside? It's bitterly cold today."

"I'm sorry, Kasey," he cleared his throat, "this is a crime scene."

The ladies' eyes widened to the point where they looked more like saucers than eyes. Another lady said, "We demand to see Mr. Prescott. He's our neighbor, and we want to make sure he's all right."

"Barbara, there's been an accident. That's all I can say. I'm sure there will be an official statement soon. How about we step outside and talk?"

The third woman thrust her chin up and glared at him. "We have nothing to say to you, Eddie Jacobs. Acting all high and mighty." They locked arms and marched down the steps.

He shook his head and closed the door. Before he turned around, he took several deep breaths. His shoulders rose and fell with each inhale and exhale. "Julie Clinton has always been the ringleader of those three, even in school."

"It figures Kasey Pelham, Barbara Hall, and Julie Clinton would stick their noses in." Beth said, "You'll need to talk with them separately if you hope to get pertinent information."

"That's what I'm afraid of." He turned, but I saw the sadness in his eyes momentarily. There must be more to him than a schoolyard bully and a cop. It was clear Beth and Eddie knew each other; maybe she'd shed some light on the situation later.

The door burst open, and Ethan rushed in. "Girls, what's happened? I got here as fast as I could, are you hurt?"

"Dad, we're fine." Beth allowed him to fold his arms around her. "When we arrived, Claudia came inside and discovered Mr. Prescott dead. It's been crazy ever since. It seems someone reported a gunshot. There was a revolver on the floor, and it might be the murder weapon."

Keeping his arm around Beth, he said, "Eddie, I'm taking the girls back to the dress shop. When you're ready to question them, call me. I'll bring them to the station." His voice didn't leave room for discussion. He took my hand, pulled me up from the stairs, and looked me in the eyes. "I'll follow you."

I hesitated, unsure if I should go with Ethan and Beth or stay and face whatever music was yet to be played. Since witnessing the officer's moment of vulnerability in his demeanor, I softened my opinion and thought of him as Officer Eddie.

He gave us a curt nod. "You can leave."

I walked around him and down the steps, without a backward glance. His gaze burned into my back. I hurried to keep up with Ethan and Beth.

Officer Amos held up a hand to stop us.

"Ethan, thanks for coming down." He nodded to me and Beth. "The ladies could use a calming presence. They've had quite the fright."

He wasn't kidding. It was my very first real, live dead body. I winced at how wrong those words were, but I didn't care. It felt good to ramble, even if it was an internal monologue. And why was Officer Amos being nice now?

"What can you tell me?" Ethan stood tall with his head held high, his presence commanding. It was easy to picture him as an officer.

"We got a report of a gunshot at ten. When we arrived, Beth and Ms. Grant were inside, and Ms. Grant was holding a gun in her hand near the body."

"I told Officer Amos that when I touched Mr. Prescott's hand it was cold, and then we heard a door bang near the back. As I stepped around the body, I kicked something solid under a chair. When I retrieved it, I discovered it was a gun."

Ethan's brow arched. "The body was cold?"

I nodded. "It must be because the house was cold."

"What's the temperature of the house?"

Amos said, "We haven't checked yet, but I know what you think. The thermostat was adjusted."

"Is that an important clue?" I looked from Amos to Ethan to Beth.

She shrugged her shoulders. "Search me."

Ethan gave Amos a stern look. "I told Eddie I'll bring the girls down when you're ready to talk with them, and to be crystal clear, I *will* be in the room when you do."

Amos nodded. "Got it."

He stepped back and allowed us to pass as we walked to my Jeep. Ethan waited until we were inside with the engine running before he tapped Beth's window.

She eased it down. "Not to worry, we're going straight to the shop."

"Drive careful, Claudia."

I pulled away from the curb and noticed the three women in a small cluster near the edge of the lawn. "Is everyone in a small town always curious about what's happening to their neighbors?"

"They are." Beth waved. "You're looking at the fastest grapevine in the country. By now, most of the town will know that something has happened to Prescott, and we're in the thick of it."

I sighed. "Me more than you. This isn't the welcome wagon my grandmother always talked about."

6

____

I paced the shop from the front windows to the back room. Ethan and Beth sat on one of the sofas, waiting silently. Finally, I flopped down and groaned. "They think I killed him, don't they?"

Ethan's voice was devoid of emotion. "If I were the cop on the scene, you'd be my prime suspect, but the evidence won't support it long term."

I sat up. "Was the body stiff because the house was cold?"

He didn't flinch. "My estimate, Prescott had been dead for twelve to twenty-four hours."

I thought for a moment, and my eyes widened. "Someone is trying to set me up?"

Beth leaned forward and grabbed my hand. "It appears that way, but don't worry, Dad and I are standing beside you."

"She's right. We're in your corner. However, it's not a coincidence that he was murdered after contacting you about buying the shop and lying about your uncle agreeing to sell. I'm jumping to a conclusion, but whoever was responsible for Herman's death may have killed Prescott. We know Herman died after a bad fall."

Lola trotted into the room, and I looked around. "How did you get in here?" I jumped up and hurried to the back stairs. The interior door leading to my apartment was ajar. I wrenched it open and peered up the passageway. The door at the top was closed. "I'll be right back." I felt compelled to check it out. The nagging urge to go upstairs was something I couldn't explain.

Beth joined me. "I'm coming with you."

Ethan was behind her. "Let me go first."

"It's okay, I've got this." I reminded myself that Nancy Drew always led the way. As we crept upward, my heart thudded in my chest. I touched the knob and eased the door open an inch at a time. Peering through the widening crack, the apartment was still. Sunlight streamed in the kitchen from the living room windows. The open floor plan was conducive to seeing most of the space simultaneously. Lola squeezed past me when I was in the kitchen and trotted ahead.

I slipped off my sneakers to move as quietly as possible. The living room was tidy, exactly the way I had left it earlier. I tiptoed down the hall to my bedroom. Beth was on my heels, and Ethan was looking over Cade Street from the front windows.

The bedroom door stood open, and everything looked the same. As I turned to leave, I paused and tipped my head. Pointing to the closet door they were cracked. I pressed my finger to my lips. Beth nodded. I skirted to the side of the wardrobe before I flung it open. I half-expected someone to jump out. Thankfully, that didn't happen. However, someone shoved the hangers to one end of the rod, and kicked the shoes out of their neat rows.

I patted my pants pocket, but my phone wasn't there. "Beth, can I borrow your phone with the flashlight?"

She handed it to me. "What are you looking for?"

"I'm not sure, but with luck, I'll know when I see it." Mimicking what I had seen in a movie, I started at the now-empty end and ran the light over the wall, tapping it to see if it sounded hollow. I moved down the wall and pushed the clothes to the other end before stepping back. "Nothing."

I fixed the hangers so I wouldn't have to iron all my clothes and ignored the shoe mess; that was a project for later. I heard a tap on the bathroom door from the hall. The door from my room to the bath was open. "Ethan, we're in my room."

He strode in as his cheeks flushed a subtle pink. "Sorry. I like to be thorough."

"So far, nothing. All that's left is Herman's room." I scanned my room and walked into the hall. Where was my friendly ghost hiding?

I finished tiptoeing around my apartment and opened the last door.

Herman perched in the middle of his bed with his head hanging low. He looked up.

More importantly, an intruder had ransacked his room.

"What happened in here?" It wasn't possible to address Herman, but he knew I was talking to him.

"I was downstairs when Lola strolled in like she owned the shop. I never let her have full access to make sure she didn't use any bolts of fabric as a bed. She swished her tail and went to the bottom of the stairs. When I got here, I found this. Whoever was here finished but left this a disaster."

Ethan said, "I'm calling this in. Don't touch anything."

"Is it necessary? I can tidy the room and call it a day."

"Claudia, someone breaking into your home on the same day you're to meet with a man who was already dead is not a random act of bad luck."

Herman said, "He's right. Let Ethan help you."

Beth slipped her arm around my shoulders. "Let's go in the other room while Dad calls the station."

"I'm starting to question whether I should have moved to Drakes Bay. All of this feels overwhelming." The weight of my future hung heavy on my shoulders. "I yearned for a nice, simple life: sewing, community involvement, and forming genuine friendships. Was that too much?"

Beth guided me to the sofa. I buried my head in my hands. The gentle, cool breeze from Herman joining me was comforting, while Beth sat on the opposite side. Lola perched on my feet and purred.

"You belong here, Claudia. Not to sound like an old codger, but you need to start thinking about what's happening. Use your brain. Think of this as a final exam, and researching clues is studying. If you don't help the police discover the why behind all of this, the reason for my death will go unsolved."

"This might not make sense to anyone, including me." I looked at Beth. "I want Herman to get the justice he deserves. Now that I'm a reluctant participant in not one but two murders and a break-in, I'm going to look at the problem, search for clues, and see if I can discover details that the police overlooked. Especially since someone seems to think something in my apartment is important."

Beth glanced over her shoulder. "Dad wouldn't be comfortable if you went off on your own looking for answers." She dropped her voice. "I'll help if you let me. We can be like Nancy Drew and Beth, instead of Bess." When I furrowed my brow, she said, "What? It works."

Following her attempt to lighten the mood, I said, "Maybe we're better as Cagney and Lacey minus being cops."

With a shrug, she said, "At least we're both creative in different ways. We're mirror images of the other's talents like Cagney and Lacey."

I smiled. "Instead, how about we become the B and C team? Create our own partnership."

"I like it." Beaming, she stuck out her hand. "Partner."

I gave it a shake. "Partner. Our first step will be to develop a clue document. I can do that on my phone and share it with you."

Rubbing her hands together, she grinned. "A top-secret murder board. Sweet."

Herman said, "That's not exactly what I meant."

I laughed at him and Beth. "Exactly." I said, "My phone's downstairs, I'll be right back." I raced down the steps and back up; out of breath, I sat down.

Ethan joined us. "Eddie will be over as soon as he can. I told him we'll sit tight and wait." He looked from me to Beth. "What are you two conspiring?"

I gave Beth a wink. "Nothing—except we've been talking about what's happened. How do you think the person gained access to the apartment?"

"I'm about to find out." He pointed to the back door. "I'll check to make sure that door's locked, then I'll go down the back stairs and through the front."

I got up. "I'm going with you. If someone is coming and going as they please, I want to know how, so I'll be on alert."

He gave me a grudging nod. "You have a point. Just look while I poke around."

I jammed my hands in my pockets. "You have my word."

Ethan said, "Well then, let's go."

"Wait, I need boots." I zipped down the hall to my bedroom and stepped into my boots before returning to grab my coat.

Beth and I trailed behind him. I mimed like I was jotting something down. She seemed to understand I'd capture this in our new digital note later.

Ethan knelt on the floor and studied the lock. "Looks good from this side." He flipped the lock, pulled open the door, and repeated the same inspection of the outside handle. "Nothing to see here."

I photographed both sides of the door and followed Ethan down the stairs. A little snow had blown onto them overnight, and I made a mental note to keep them brushed off for any guests who might stop by.

When we reached the bottom, Ethan scanned the area. He walked to the inn next door and traversed the length of the alley between us. I pointed to the boot prints in the snow that led from the town hall. Again, while taking pictures, I bent down to capture a close-up of the tread. If they did that on television, it must be a good idea. I turned toward the door and noticed the same boot print coming off the back step and moving between my building and the inn next door. "We can see how he came and went." I grabbed Beth's arm. "Look at the scratches around the knob and lock."

"We should let Dad see this before we open the door."

I agreed. My heart thumped in my chest.

"Dad, you'd better have a look."

He stayed clear of the footprints. "What did you find?"

I pointed to the tracks leading between the buildings. "He left, walking to the street."

"Bold," he muttered under his breath.

"And the lock's been jimmied." I had taken pictures of the prints and the lock before Ethan made it back. Now it was time to see what he thought.

"Excellent observation. The lock has been tampered with." His cell rang. "Stewart." He nodded. "Right. We'll meet you out front." He secured the phone on the holder at his waist. "That was Eddie. Let's leave this area and go through the shop via the apartment. Eddie will be there by the time we get out front, and we can fill him in on what's happened."

"It's too bad Officer Amos isn't coming. At the end of our conversation, he was less hostile than Officer Jacobs."

"Claudia, Eddie's a good cop. He grew up here and worked in Albany, New York, for a few years before moving back. While he was there, he saw a lot. The adjustment to small-town police work has been a relief and a challenge."

"Do small town politics come into play for the police department?"

Beth snorted. "Sure, everyone knows everyone else and is friends with everyone. Which is why you're under suspicion since you're new."

"That's just swell." I tromped up the stairs beside Beth, and Ethan was in front of us.

He glanced over his shoulder. "Don't worry. Before you know it, you won't be the new girl in town. Someone else will move in."

"That's something to look forward to." We made a beeline for the stairs leading to the shop. Once in the main salon, I saw Eddie standing at the shop door, hands cupped around his eyes, trying to peer in.

I opened the door. "Officer Jacobs, thank you for coming so quickly."

He looked me over, taking in my snow-covered boots and jacket, which hung open, and then he studied my face. "Ms. Grant. We meet again. I'll admit I expected to see you at the station. Not here."

"Eddie, play nice. An unknown person entered Claudia's apartment via the back entrance. She's the victim, not the criminal."

He looked at me. "That remains to be seen, but tell me what happened, and then show me."

"When we returned from Mr. Prescott's, Beth, Ethan, and I were in here," I gestured toward the sofas, "when Lola strolled in. The doors to the interior stairs were secure before I left. There was no way she could have gotten into the dress shop."

"Maybe you forgot to close them."

I didn't like the smug look or condescending tone in his voice. "Not possible. I know that door was closed."

Beth said, "I can vouch that the lower door is always closed."

"That's convenient."

"Eddie." Ethan's tone carried a distinct warning. "We don't treat every citizen as if they're guilty and have to prove their innocence. That pressure tactic might work in a city but not here."

He shuffled his feet. "Continue, Ms. Grant."

"As I was saying, Lola was in the shop. We went upstairs to check my apartment. My bedroom closet had been searched, and my uncle's former bedroom was ransacked. I can't tell if anything is missing. That's when Ethan mentioned we should call you." I hated that I had to give him a blow-by-blow of the last half hour, but with some luck, it would help him see he had misjudged me.

"Ethan, I'm sure you've poked around."

"There are footprints in the snow leading to the back door from the alley between the store and the inn and then to the street via the town hall. The lock on the door has been tampered with." He held up his hand. "Before you insinuate that Claudia is mistaken: Two days ago, I changed the locks on all the doors, and the lock was pristine. I wish I had gotten the security cameras installed."

"Show me what you found, and I'll file a report." He gave me a curt nod. "Off the record, Ms. Grant, it seems you've unwittingly walked into a tangled mess. Maybe you should cut your losses and leave town before you get hurt."

I lifted my chin and declared more confidently than I felt, "I don't run from problems, Officer Jacobs. I solve them."

7

$\mathcal{I}$ trailed behind Eddie Jacobs as Ethan walked him through my apartment, down the outside stairs, and showed him the back door. He slipped on a pair of latex gloves and turned the knob. I was gobsmacked when I realized it wasn't locked. "I know the door was locked when Beth and I left."

The officer raised his eyebrows and placed his hands on his holster. "Ms. Grant. If someone went to the trouble of picking the lock, then it stands to reason they succeeded. And before you ask, most likely, they entered the building through this door."

I didn't appreciate the snide tone, and I wasn't going to ask. He was a friend of Ethan's and an acquaintance of Beth's, so I held the sharp retort that longed to spring from my lips, *Of course they went through this door.* "Can we go in and see if anything was searched? Earlier, we were in the main room until we went upstairs."

"Stay behind me." He opened the door and looked over his shoulder. "At a safe distance?"

I flashed a questioning glance at Beth. What was that, and

why had this cop taken an instant dislike to me? I was an innocent pawn in whatever game being played.

She shrugged, and I let Ethan go first. He'd keep the required distance from Eddie Jacobs.

I hadn't noticed when we were outside, but Eddie held a flashlight, sweeping the bright beam around the room's interior. Once I walked inside, I breathed a sigh of relief. The room was just as I had left it—the opposite of Herman's room. Whatever they had been looking for, they hadn't thought it was in the store. It was a means to enter the building.

"Ms. Grant?"

"Call me Claudia." This Ms. Grant stuff had gotten old.

He gave a curt nod as if he would in the future. "Nothing seems out of place?"

"I know it looks messy, but I haven't had time to organize the heart of the business. I concentrated on the apartment first. At the end of a busy day, it's best to go home to a serene space and unwind." Why did I bother to include that last detail? It wasn't necessary.

He slowly left the workroom, checking each dressing room and then the main salon. "Is there a basement?"

I shook my head. "I have no idea. Ethan?"

"There is. Come with me." He went back into the workroom and stood next to a wall of fabric. "There's a panel here. If you press it, the door opens." As he spoke, he moved a bolt of cloth and pushed it against the wall. In front of me, a door opened.

"It's like a secret passage," Beth said. "How come I don't have one in my shop?"

My laugh was a nervous twitter. "What's next, nighty-nine steps?"

Eddie gave me a sharp look. "Basements typically have between twelve or sixteen, depending on the ceiling height. If it's a crawl space for utilities only, less."

"That's an obscure factoid, Eddie." Beth gave me a wink. She seemed pleased to have the opportunity to tease the man.

I'd have to get the skinny on what was between the two.

"Beth, I'm not a dumb jock."

Ethan cleared his throat. "Is anyone curious to check out the basement?"

I raised a hand like a schoolgirl. "Me."

Once again, Eddie led the way, his flashlight beam trained on the steps.

Ethan reached around the doorway and snapped on a light. "That should help."

The sound of Eddie's boots hitting the solid stairs gave me hope I wasn't looking at a space that needed repairs. A cool, feather-like breeze fluttered over my cheek. I looked behind me and Herman drifted into the room.

"Beth, go in front of me. I'll be right behind you. I just need a moment to settle my nerves."

She placed a comforting hand on my shoulder. "I'll stay with you."

"No, really. Go on, I'll be down in a second."

She searched my face before going through the doorway.

"Herman, what is going on?"

"Besides the obvious that someone keeps breaking into our property looking for something?"

"What is it?"

His filmy form shrugged. "I don't know. If I did, I'd tell you, but I just wanted to give you a heads-up about the basement."

"Oh?"

"You'll need to maintain the temperature and humidity down there. I have a wine cellar and store some antique lace and leather. Nothing I use in the shop, but the environment must be carefully controlled."

"Couldn't you have told me this after everyone leaves?"

"I didn't want you flipping any switches when you get down to save a few pennies on the utility bill."

"I'll leave everything alone, and *we will talk later*." I put extra emphasis on the second half of my sentence. I moved cautiously down the polished wooden steps. *Pretty fancy for a basement.* Partway down, the stairs curved to the right, and I paused mid-descent. Before me was a luxurious room. An overstuffed sofa and four recliner chairs faced a large screen on one wall, a bar with four stools, and plush carpeting covered the floor. "This isn't an ordinary basement."

"Herman was a movie buff but always seemed to miss showtime. One day, I joked he should install a movie theater in the cellar. He took my suggestion to heart and created this space so he could watch movies whenever he wanted. Often, I'd join him. Those recliners are the best for a movie marathon."

There was so much I didn't know about Herman. How come my grandmother hadn't told me? "It looks like a fun space to have a party. Is there a storage room?"

Ethan gestured to another door under the stairs. "Right through there. Herman had all repairmen come through the outside hatch when it was time to service the HVAC system."

"Good to know." I came down the last few steps. Eddie opened the storage room door before I could get there.

He frowned. "You're first after me."

I was curious about the controlled space for the lace and leather Herman had mentioned and the wine cellar. The floor was cement, and off to one side was the utility area.

"You haven't been down here?"

"No." I looked around and noticed two doors. That must be what I was looking for.

He pointed the flashlight at the opposite wall. "There's the circuit breaker box," he said, focusing the beam on a valve. "The water shutoff is over there."

"Thanks. That's good to know."

. . .

"Y ou should keep a flashlight at the top of the stairs. If you'd like, I can attach one to the wall."

"Officer Jacobs, are you being nice to me?"

He gave me a pointed look. "I'd rather not be called back for an emergency like you taking a tumble down the steps if the power goes out."

"Thank you. I'm sure Ethan will help." I tipped my head. "Is that why you're beginning to show you've got a heart under that badge? To protect and serve the newest member of town?"

He snorted. "I have a heart. It doesn't bleed for criminals, and before you think you've convinced me that you're innocent, Ethan is the best judge of people I know. You couldn't hoodwink him. If he says you didn't kill Prescott, then I believe him."

"Will Officer Amos agree with you despite the evidence?"

"That's not for me to say. Let me do my job and finish checking the area."

I stepped back and pointed to the closed doors. "I believe that might be two climate-controlled areas, one for fabric and the other for wine."

He cocked a brow. "How do you know about them if you didn't know about the basement?"

I couldn't confess that a ghost told me. I crossed my fingers behind my back. "My grandmother was Herman's sister-in-law, and she mentioned in passing that he was a collector of wine and antique fabrics, and both have to be in climate-controlled areas. It's the only logical place since I haven't seen any other likely areas."

He gave me another assessing look. There was no reason he shouldn't believe me. It was a perfectly plausible answer. "You should ask her if Herman planned on selling the shop."

"I can assure you he wasn't. The plan was always for me

to come and work with him and someday take over." I gestured to the doors. "Can we open them? I'm dying to see what's inside."

He flicked the switch next to the door and turned the knob pulling open the first frosted glass door. "Wine." He entered and gave a low whistle. "I'm an amateur enthusiast, and he's got an excellent collection."

I followed him into the small room. The floor was polished walnut, wooden racks lined three walls and each cubby held a bottle. In the center of the room were two upholstered leather chairs, a small table between them with a corkscrew, and four glasses turned upside down. "It's as if he was expecting to walk in and enjoy wine with a friend."

Eddie cleared his throat. "It's impressive, but nothing seems to be out of place. Whoever got into the shop didn't come down here. A word of caution; if you come down here, make sure you have your phone and that the door at the top of the stairs is propped open. It wouldn't be fun to get locked in." He withdrew his cell. "There's a strong signal."

"That would stink." I suppressed the shiver that raced over me. "Ready for the fabric room?"

Eddie nodded. We followed the same process. He opened the door and went in first. The room wasn't as fancy as the wine room, but it had the same flooring, and one wall had shelves with stacks of lace and a few leather pieces. I sighed. "It's tidy in here."

Herman appeared in the room. "There's a wall safe under the leather. But I don't remember the combination."

I couldn't acknowledge what he said. Instead, I walked to the small stack of supple leather and pulled it from the shelf, pretending I concentrated on the material while searching for the safe.

Eddie said, "What are you doing?"

"I'm curious to know what type of leather this is." As I

went to slide it back on the shelf, I said, "Hello, look, there's a safe."

"Did you know about that?" He tugged on the handle. "Do you have the code?

I shook my head. "No, but I'll ask my grandmother. Herman may have told her. Or maybe it's with the legal papers. I can ask Ethan."

I stepped into the movie room. "Ethan, do you know if Uncle Herman left the combination to a safe in his will?"

He pursed his lips. "Not that I recall, but we can contact his lawyer tomorrow. I guess you found one?"

"Yes, it's a keypad." I did my best to control my breathing. Everything that had happened today, including Prescott, the discovery of the wine cellar, the movie room, and now the safe had my heart racing. There were so many reasons for Person X to want to break in.

"Herman was very meticulous, I'm sure he left it with his paperwork. Don't worry. I'll make the appointment, and we can find out. If not, we can call a locksmith to open it. There are a couple of good ones in the area."

Eddie followed me. "I've secured both doors and turned the lights off. Since there's nothing else to see here, we should go upstairs. I'll need to return to the station to finish this paperwork after I check the apartment."

"I appreciate your help."

"Ms. Grant." His eyes softened. "Claudia. It's my job."

In the last few hours, Eddie Jacobs had gone from treating me like a killer, suspecting me of nefarious deeds, to believing I was a person who had unwittingly walked into a mess. And the man was easy on the eyes, to boot.

"Ethan. Could you install deadbolts on the exterior doors in addition to the cameras? If you don't have time to finish it today, I'll ask the night patrolman to make a couple of extra drive-bys and even pull in behind the building just to make sure no one's loitering."

"Not to worry," Beth had been quiet during the search. "I'm staying with her tonight, and if it's okay with you, Officer, we should go through Herman's room to see if there is any clue as to why someone broke in again. Ransacking it after Herman died was one thing, but after Claudia arrived is disconcerting."

Ethan said, "That's not a bad idea. I'm not waiting for the weather to cooperate to install the locks and camera. By the time I get supplies, I won't be able to finish today."

"I'm off at four. I can swing by and give you a hand."

Beth narrowed her eyes. "Are you trying to make up for the fact you originally accused Claudia of killing Mr. Prescott?"

"I never said she did or didn't. I treat all witnesses as potentially guilty."

She poked him in the arm. "Eddie, the law states innocence first."

He looked at his arm and her finger and then winked at me when Beth turned her back. "Assaulting an officer of the law can get you arrested."

"Not if he's your cousin." She stomped up the stairs.

I stammered, "Cousin?"

He shrugged. "Ethan's my mom's brother."

Ethan's eyes twinkled. "You can trust this big lug."

I crossed my arms over my chest. "Is Amos related to you, too?"

"Nope, he's a newcomer. He's only a second-generation Mainer."

"Right. Claudia mentioned that you needed three generations deep to be considered local."

"Not to worry, we're a welcoming bunch. Especially as a shop owner." He swept his arm to the stairs. "After you."

I had ping-pong-itis. I wanted to curl up on the sofa with a cup of tea, a plate of decadent cookies, and a blanket and mull over everything that had transpired. Hopefully, Beth was up for the do nothing but think approach, too.

Ethan pulled his gloves on as Eddie secured the basement door and slid the fabric panel in place.

"Can you add a wall-mount flashlight to your list? I told Claudia I'd put one up for her."

"Sure." He clapped his hands together. "Eddie, I'll meet you back here around four?"

"You bet." He smiled, "Beth, any chance you could whip up dinner? Spaghetti would hit the spot. I'll look at Herman's room before I go and have questions for Claudia later."

It sounded like it was natural for Eddie to invite himself for dinner.

Beth said, "Don't you think waiting to be asked is the polite thing to do?"

"It's okay, Beth. It'll be nice to have people here." I glanced around the shop and shivered. "Maybe it will keep the burglar away if they are watching the place and see everyone coming and going."

Eddie's smile charmed me right down to my toes. "Great idea. Dinner."

I nodded. Hosting an impromptu dinner was at the top of my list. Right after I cleaned Herman's room, tried to find time to bake a batch of cookies, and make notes about Herman and Mr. Prescott's murders.

8

$\mathcal{B}$eth pushed the top drawer of the dresser in. "I'm glad Eddie was cool with us putting this room back together. But, Claudia, your grandmother never said anything about Herman dying under mysterious circumstances?"

"Grammie said he died from a fall and hit his head. Now that I think about it, she thought the police officer who called was a bit vague." I perched on the side of the bed. "She wouldn't have encouraged me to move here if she thought there was any danger."

"Of course not. There was no reason for her to know anyone would come snooping around, either." Her eyes grew wide. "What if whoever it was had a key and was coming and going since Herman died? Searching for whatever."

I narrowed my eyes and scanned the room. "If we could determine what Person X is looking for, we could figure out the why. I wish Uncle Herman left us a clue."

"There's his appointment book." Excitement laced Beth's voice and I knew exactly how she felt.

"We can't tell your family what we're doing."

Sticking out her pinky, I wrapped mine around hers. She said, "Deal."

She folded the patchwork quilt and placed it at the foot of the bed. A lump rose in my throat knowing Herman wouldn't ever sleep under it again. "Thanks for your help. This is a little overwhelming, and I haven't even had time to think about reopening the shop, yet."

"Tomorrow's a new day." She pulled me up from the bed. "We have just enough time to scan the date book while I put a pot of sauce and meatballs on simmer if you have ingredients in the cabinet."

I shook my head. "I need a quick trip to the market. The pantry has canned soup, tuna, crackers, and peanut butter, and the freezer has four pints of freezer-burned ice cream and two trays of ice cubes."

She tapped her finger to the chin. "Yeah, what Dad picked up won't constitute dinner, either. Come on. We'll go to the market, and I can introduce you to Polly Elliot, the owner. If there are any specialty items she doesn't carry, you can ask her to stock them. If it's possible, she will."

"That's awfully accommodating of her. Why would she do that?" We walked down the hall.

"Two reasons. She wants to keep our business in town. Other folks might want to purchase it, too, so it increases her sales overall."

"Smart businesswoman." I handed Beth her jacket and eased Lola off mine. She rolled over, showing her tummy, and looked at me through narrow slits in her eyes. I obliged the unspoken request for a quick belly rub. Herman had joined us and took his usual spot on the windowsill.

She smiled at me. "I've never seen Lola take to anyone as quickly as she has you."

Herman said, "I told her you were a good person, and you'd care for her."

"I'm sure it's because I feed her and let her sleep on the bed with me." I smiled at Herman's ghost.

"Cats are an excellent judge of character." She zipped her coat and adjusted her knit hat. "Ready?"

I shut the door closed by pulling it and pushed to confirm it locked. The last thing we needed was to return and discover an unwanted guest. I tucked the collar of my jacket close to my chin. "That wind is cutting."

"You need a scarf. How did you get along in the city without proper outerwear?" Beth grinned. "It's a good thing you've got a friend who has access to wool."

"I can't knit, but give me a sewing machine, and I'm a whiz." We tromped down the wooden steps. "Do we need to drive to the market?"

"It's just over the next street, and Polly will let us take a shopping cart back if you get carried away shopping." She jostled my shoulder as we reached the bottom. "This is small-town living at its best."

The day's cold seemed to absorb into my bones as we crossed the street.

Beth waved to a car and truck, which stopped as we crossed. She nodded, "You'll get to know the locals soon enough. I expect people will drop by once the shop is open, and the inquisition will commence."

"What do you mean? They're not thrilled with a dress shop in town?"

"On the contrary. The new owner is what's the draw." She laughed softly. "Don't worry. Everyone's nice. Well, except for whoever is responsible for Herman and Prescott."

She pulled open an old-fashioned glass-and-wood door. We entered a quaint market that looked more like something from the mid-century than now. There were four checkout lines, with one register attended. A young woman smiled at Beth.

"Hey, Polly. This is Claudia Grant, Herman's great niece. She's going to reopen the dress shop."

Coming around the end of the counter, she thrust her hand to me and pumped my arm. "Welcome to Drakes Bay. I'm very sorry about your uncle. Herman Grant was a special man and loved his ice cream."

Polly's warm welcome was like Beth's when we met a few days ago. "Thank you, Polly. I guessed he did since I noticed a few freezer-burned pints stashed in the refrigerator. It's not a full shop today, just a few things for dinner and some items for baking."

"Whatever you need. Oh, and if you need a cart to get items to your place, that's fine, too." Again, she smiled. "But I'm sure Beth already mentioned that."

"She did. Thank you for the kind offer." I took a cart from the stack and trailed behind Beth, who seemed to be on a mission. Then again, she knew where everything was for our dinner.

We rounded a corner, and I ran into Amos Branson, cart first. "Officer, I beg your pardon." I stepped back, and my face flushed with color. I wasn't making a good impression on the police department today. If I kept this up, he might consider me a serious threat to the town.

"No harm done, Ms. Grant."

"Beth is showing me around and introduced me to Polly." I didn't need to explain to him why I was in a food market.

He looked past me and nodded. "Polly's got a nice store here. I haven't forgotten about continuing our conversation from earlier, but the day's been unexpectedly complicated. Can you come to the police station at nine tomorrow?"

Beth appeared next to me. "Absolutely."

I bobbed my head as my mouth dried out.

"Good. Beth, I assume you will be accompanying Claudia. I have questions for you, as well."

Her eyes narrowed. "Of course. Dad, too." She nodded to

the butcher counter. "Come on, Claudia. We need some ground meat."

The air sparked with tension, but I wasn't sure what had just happened. Earlier today she'd been curt with him. But he seemed amiable enough. Eddie had been the hardnose cop on the scene, and after spending a bit of time with him in my basement, we had come to an understanding of sorts.

Beth hissed out a breath. "Don't look now."

Of course, I turned in the direction she was looking. Three women were pushing carts in our direction. Who were they? Then, it dawned on me that they were the women who lived in Mr. Prescott's neighborhood.

"Beth. We haven't been introduced to our newest resident."

"Claudia Grant, this is Kasey Pelham, Julie Clinton, and Barbara Hall. They are on various committees in town but spend more time at the spa or shopping."

"You make it sound like we're bottom dwellers of the ocean." The one she called Kasey shook my hand. Her grip was like a limp chiffon fabric.

"Welcome to Drakes Bay," Julie said. "What were you doing at Prescott's this morning? He never sees anyone."

Barbara leaned forward. "Did you kill him or find him already dead?" The gleam in her eye was unnerving.

Beth clamped a hand on my arm. "Claudia hasn't given her full statement to the police yet. I'm sure you understand she's not at liberty to gossip."

Barbara glared at her. "We're not gossiping. If a murderer is running loose in our neighborhood, we should know so that we can protect ourselves.

With a snort, Beth said, "There's not a single group of people in town better equipped to thwart anyone who comes to your doors. All you'd need to do is talk until they get bored and leave."

"Beth Stewart, you take that back." Julie stomped her foot.

Was I witnessing a minor temper tantrum?

"Truth hurt, ladies?"

Kasey tossed her long red hair over her shoulder. "Typical. Beth thinks she knows everything, but we'll have the last laugh. Your new BFF is in deep trouble if Amos won't clear her of suspicion."

"Wait, won't or can't?" I looked at the four women. "I'm innocent."

Barbara said, "Just like every other criminal, feigning innocence."

Kasey turned, and the other two followed her. "What did I witness, the sequel to *Mean Girls*"?

Beth waited until they had gone around the corner before she leaned closer to me. "They're harmless for the most part. They just think they're special. I hate to admit it, but in their defense, they do great volunteer work; the rest of the time, they're a pain in the backside. They think they should be informed when someone sneezes in town."

"I'll boldly say they won't become regulars in my shop."

"On the contrary. They'll shop to have great clothes and try to get the skinny on your customers—who's getting married or whatever else they want to know. For women like that, it's their mission in life to get the deets."

"I wish I had taken their pictures at the crime scene this morning. Since they were there, I'm going to consider them suspects. And they're the only three on my list so far; it would have been a good reference point."

Passing me the grocery basket, she said, "Stay right here."

A few minutes later, she sauntered up the aisle and gave me a saucy wink. "Pictures secured, CG."

"Huh?" She was calling me by my initials now. What the heck was going on? I felt like I had stepped off a tilt-a-whirl ever since I got to town.

"If we're going to emulate that famous sleuth Nancy Drew and her friends, we need code names for when we're in detective mode. You should be CG, and I'll be Bess instead of Beth."

"You thought of that on the spur of the moment? And I thought we were emulating Cagney and Lacey."

"Nah. Besides, I've been noodling them for a bit since we decided to investigate what's happened with Herman, the break-ins at your place, and Prescott. You're right—somehow, it's all related."

I agreed with her, but a public market wasn't the place to discuss our plan. I nodded. "Now, about that ground meat." I gave her a wink and touched my ear, hoping she'd understand that I was concerned someone might be listening to our conversation.

"Right, and we'll pick up Italian sausage, too."

*B*ack at my apartment, I stowed the groceries while Beth tossed ingredients for sauce, the meatballs, and sausage links in an oversized pot. I brewed tea and grabbed the box of maple cookies I had picked up at the store —so much for baking. We took what I was beginning to think of as our spots in the living room. Herman was sitting in a rocking chair, with Lola curled on his lap. If I hadn't seen my friendly ghost, I would have thought Lola preferred to sit alone rather than with me.

I opened my phone's notes app. "We need to go back to when Herman died."

Beth curled her legs underneath her and nibbled on a cookie. "Right, to figure out why Prescott wanted to buy this building. That's the start of all of this."

I jumped up, hurried to the kitchen, retrieved the date-book, and settled back on the sofa. "We know that Herman and Prescott talked, and that Herman got the documentation to prove he was the rightful owner."

"Which was never really in doubt, but Herman went the

extra step to prove his point. Is it possible that Prescott only wanted this place because he could make a buck? Take advantage of a lonely old man?"

"Who's she calling old?" Herman mumbled from the rocking chair.

I ignored his comment. "If that was the case, then why has someone broken in after Prescott was murdered? There must be something else. We need to skip ahead to the Prescott issue." I got up and paced in front of the windows overlooking the street. "He called me last night and confirmed the time of the meeting. If he had been shot this morning, would his body have been cold and stiff? How long does that take to happen? Remember, the house was chilly."

"Dad said twelve to twenty-four hours. Do you remember what time he called the first time? That would give us a starting point of when he was still alive."

"Ethan had just returned with the groceries, maybe around four? Thirty-six hours plus from the first phone call before I was supposed to meet him, which indicates he was alive when he called me."

"Add that to a timeline."

Herman said, "Write it in the back of the datebook. No one will think to look there."

Following his suggestion, I took it from the side table and made the notes. "Can you double-check how long it takes for a body to get cold? Not that I doubt your dad, but confirming our information is important."

She tapped a few keys on her phone. "Confirming what Dad said, twelve to twenty-four hours, but ambient room temperature can change that, and the room was cold, so it could be as long as thirty-six hours."

I wrote that down. "Let's say he was killed late yesterday after he confirmed our meeting. Whoever called in the gunshot lied." I got up again and paced to the window. More to myself than to Beth, I said, "Amos said the call came in at ten. But Prescott was cold and stiff and had to have been killed yesterday. Someone knew I had an appointment with him this morning, and calling in the reported sound of a gunshot made me the prime suspect."

Beth cleared her throat. "I hate to point out the obvious, but you're the only suspect."

9

I sank to the window seat. "Once the body is examined, they'll know when he died and that I couldn't possibly have shot him." I saw worry lines etched around Beth's mouth and eyes. Or was that doubt on her face?

"Beth, you don't think I killed that man, do you?"

"There isn't a doubt in my mind of your innocence, but Amos Branson isn't the most detail-focused cop on the force. I wished Eddie had shown up first."

"They didn't come together?"

"They each had a patrol car. Amos must have been closer when the call came in. The first cop on the scene takes the lead."

"It's too bad he wasn't downtown and saw whoever was coming out of the alley between here and the inn. At least we might have a clue who broke in."

"From the prints in the snow, it was a deep tread like a work boot. We should ask Dad if any construction companies are working close to town."

I jotted that down. "What about fishermen? Don't they wear boots on the deck of the boat?"

"The marina is down the road a couple of miles. It's possible but not likely; besides, they wear rubber boots on the boat. I'm betting it's someone who needs good tread on their footwear for their job."

I nodded thoughtfully. "Ethan would know. He's probably investigated other crime scenes with boot prints." I sipped my tea. "Tell me about the troublesome trio."

Her eyes twinkled with merriment. "That's a great name for Julie, Barbara, and Kasey. They were in school with Eddie and me, and they thought they were gifts from the gods. They ruled the school by bullying others, me included."

Herman snorted. "I remember fitting them with prom dresses. They certainly weren't angels."

"Do you think one of them could have shot Mr. Prescott? It was convenient they showed up right after the police. In the movies or on TV, the perpetrator always shows up to get their kicks and to see if the cops have a clue who did it."

"Those women are a lot of things, but killers? That's hard to wrap my head around. The gun will be tested for finger-prints, and if there's another set beside yours, that might help." She frowned.

"I know I shouldn't have touched the gun, but in my defense, I didn't expect that's what I'd find when I stuck my hand under the chair."

She waved a dismissive hand. "I get it, and I would have done the same thing. It's a reflex. We need to establish your alibi. We had dinner, and I went home at around nine. Did you talk to anyone after that? Your mom or grandmother?"

I shook my head. "I poked around a stack of papers from Herman's desk and discovered his password for the store laptop. I probably spent an hour reviewing old emails and searched for a few new vendors. Then I took a shower. It was close to eleven, so I went to bed."

Herman said, "I can vouch that she never left her bedroom all night."

I appreciated that my friendly ghost wanted to support me, but since only I could see or hear him, that wasn't helpful. Lola jumped down from the rocking chair, hopped up next to me, then rolled over on her side and began washing her paws. "It's too bad Lola can't talk. She was curled up next to me all night." I snapped my fingers. "Wait a minute. The computer will show history and time stamps. Won't that be enough proof?"

"Maybe? I wished I had stayed later or fallen asleep on the sofa, so you'd have backup." She rose from the cushions. "I need to check the sauce."

I followed her. "We're spinning in circles. We don't know why Prescott wanted this building. We don't know why someone clobbered Herman over the head and staged it to look like a bad fall. For the record, he could have fallen down the stairs. There was a narrow path between the junk. However, it's unlikely."

"I beg your pardon; it's not junk. It was all essential items I needed to keep handy, and I ran out of shelf space in the workroom.

I ignored him. "How did Prescott know I was in town? And he lied about Herman being ready to sell. Why did he call to confirm? It wasn't like it had been so long since we had set the appointment that I'd forgotten. The reported gunshot occurred around ten, and I showed up, discovered the body, and was caught holding the weapon. Lastly, someone broke in while I was away from the store and ransacked Herman's room, again." I flopped into the sofa cushions.

"Talk about an info dump." Beth held out a teaspoon with a bit of sauce. "Taste this."

I did as she requested, and my eyes widened. "That's amazing. Will there be leftovers?"

"That's the plan. I believe in cooking enough food for a few meals even when Dad and Eddie join me." She dropped the spoon in the sink and returned to the living room. "Claudia, I know you wanted to keep the clues on your phone or the date book, but it's hard for me to keep track of the moving pieces. I'm a visual person. Would you mind if we used a dry-erase board for now?"

"Do I have one of those?"

"Yes. Herman had one he used to jot ideas on at night. I'll bet it's in the entrance closet." As she talked, she went to the hallway and pushed aside some coats. "Here it is." She set it up in front of the television. "I can list your questions and write down what we know as ideas continue to spin."

"Sure, you can start." I waited while she created three columns: Prescott, Herman, and Store. Then, she added the details.

"You're right. This *is* easier to follow." I perused the list. "Add called to confirm under Prescott. I still find that odd."

Beth put the cap on the marker. "Is it possible Prescott killed Herman?"

"Maybe. But someone broke in here after Prescott was already dead." I ran my fingers through my hair and twirled the ends around my hand. "One killer. Two victims.

"Whoever killed Herman knew about the scheme Prescott had cooked up. Heck, maybe they were associates, and someone got greedy and eliminated their partner. Once I rolled into town, it sparked a new series of crimes, killing Prescott and searching Herman's room, again. Whoever this was must have thought I would go through his things and find a clue."

"I like how you're thinking. They must have guessed Dad was the estate executor. Everyone in town knew they were close."

"I don't believe that would make a difference. Once the will was probated and the property released to Herman's heir, they could make a new play for the building. This time, telling me there was an agreement in place."

Footsteps on the outside stairs drew our attention. "Quick, turn the easel around."

Beth slipped it behind the television stand just in time as I pulled open the door. "Hi, Ethan," I said it loudly enough for her to know he was alone.

"Deadbolts are in place, and there's a new lock on the back door, so it isn't all scratched up." He handed me several keys. "All labeled and ready for you to try. Also, I purchased four cameras: one for the front door, one for the back door, one covering the back parking area, and the last one for this door." He jerked his thumb over his shoulder. "They'll be connected to an app on your phone. Lastly, there's a rechargeable flashlight and holder to be installed at the top of the basement stairs. Eddie and I will finish the cameras when he gets off patrol."

He paused, drank in a deep breath, and grinned. "Homemade sauce?"

"Mom's recipe. Claudia's been the official taste tester and approved."

"What else have you ladies been up to?" His roaming gaze landed on the board.

"Tidied Herman's room and went to the market. We bumped into the troublesome trio."

His brow crinkled. "Who?"

"Kasey, Barbara, and Julie. They wanted all the salacious details about Prescott's death. This morning, they showed up and tried to push their way inside. Thankfully, Eddie stopped them."

"That's not surprising." He toed off his boots and crossed the living room. "What's this?" He eased the dry-erase board from behind the television.

"Nothing," came out of my mouth like a mouse squeak.

"Dad, it's no big deal. Claudia and I jotted down a few notes about the weird stuff that's happened."

He gave me a sharp gaze. "I don't want the two of you tracking down anything."

I was at a loss for words. Protesting our innocence sprang to mind, and those words died on my lips. "Ethan, writing down information on a board isn't the same as pulling out a magnifying glass and examining footprints. Whatever is happening, I'm up to this to my eyeballs. Before I get sucked in and charged with murder, I'd like to understand some of what's happened."

He ran a hand over his short, auburn-gray hair. "I don't like this, but show me what you've put together so far."

Beth gave me a quick thumbs-up before Ethan helped her set the board on the easel. He scanned the list and nodded.

"This isn't bad." He crossed his arms over his chest. "I didn't know Prescott called you last night. What did he want?"

"We were talking about that. He wanted to confirm our meeting time."

Ethan's brows knit together. "I thought he was clear when he called the first time?" He pulled out his phone. "I'll replay it to verify what I think we heard."

He hit the playback button on his phone, and soon, we heard the voice of the late Mr. Prescott. When the call ended, Ethan pushed a button and put his phone back in his jeans pocket.

"It was clear about the time and place." I said, "Do you find it odd he called again?"

Beth said, "It's kind of spooky hearing someone who's dead speaking."

Herman's hand went through my arm. I shivered. I wished he wouldn't do that. "Claudia, was there anything off about that second phone call compared to this one?"

A sharp rap on the door allowed me to think about Herman's question. "I'll get it."

Eddie smiled at me through the glass. Once inside, I

noticed he wore jeans, a parka, and a bright blue knit hat; he came in, stomped his snow-covered boots on the mat, and unzipped his coat. "Hey. Is Ethan here?"

"Hi. He's in the living room."

He untied his black boots and stepped out of them before entering the living room in sock-covered feet.

Ethan and Beth were talking quietly.

"What the heck is that?" Eddie's voice boomed. "Beth, don't tell me you ladies have set up a murder board."

I was behind Eddie and walked into him when he stopped short. My cheeks flushed hot. It didn't take long for this guy's temper to spike.

"It's not a murder board. Whatever that is. We just made lists about everything that's happened since I arrived, except for Herman's death."

"Ethan, are you condoning their actions? This apartment has been a train station for whoever wants to search for whatever. And yes, those vague words are perfect since we're missing critical details."

"Look, Eddie. I told Ethan we're not tracking a killer. I want to know why someone is keen on purchasing this prime piece of real estate and how killing Herman would have helped them achieve their goal. You forget I live alone. How do I know they won't come back and kill me in my sleep to get their hands on the building? I'm the last person in my family interested in running this dress shop. Wouldn't you want to know the truth if you were me?"

He looked from Beth to Ethan and finally me. "You're quite a spitfire. However, you're overlooking a key difference between us. I'm an officer trained to evaluate evidence." He tapped the board. "You've listed how long a body takes to become stiff and cold. You're trying to determine what kind of boot prints were in the snow. You've listed two phone calls and the times." He paused. "What was that about?"

I smirked. "Has our information piqued your interest, Officer?"

He frowned. "Claudia, what does that mean?"

"Beth brought dinner over yesterday, and as we were getting ready to eat, I got another call from Mr. Prescott confirming our meeting."

"What else did he say?"

"Only if he didn't answer the door to come in, he could be on a call."

"That's different from the first time he contacted you?"

"It was weird. Who calls one day apart to confirm a meeting?"

"Maybe he thought you'd change your mind. After all, he'd never met you, and from what we know, Herman didn't want to sell this building."

That was a good point, and one I hadn't thought of. "You don't think it's odd that he said to enter if he didn't answer the door?"

He gave a thoughtful nod. "I wish I had heard both calls."

Ethan said, "I recorded the first. Do you want to hear it?" He was already holding his phone.

Eddie said, "You shouldn't have."

"I didn't intend it to be used as evidence. I wanted a record that Prescott called Claudia in case he tried to pressure her into selling." Ethan pushed the button again, and this time I listened even closer to the call.

I clutched my heart as I heard him talk. Herman was right; there was something different about this call. "Guys, whoever called me last night was not Colton Prescott."

10

---

*E*ddie whirled around and faced me. His eyes locked on mine. "What do you mean it wasn't Prescott? How could you tell?"

"It was the way this man said o'clock. The *O* sounded like an *O*. But last night, I'm sure that man said *a* clock."

"Are you absolutely sure?" Ethan asked as he glanced at Eddie. "The man who called last night said *a* clock, not *o*'clock?"

My fingertips tingled. This was important to the case. "Positive."

Eddie shook his head. "Ethan, are you thinking what I'm thinking?"

I studied their expressions. They knew something. "Could Prescott have already been dead when I received the call?"

Beth gave me a sharp, questioning look as her mouth gaped open. "If he was dead, did the killer call Claudia to set her up?"

I sank into a chair. "That would make perfect sense. Someone called in a gunshot so the police would come. The house was colder than it should have been, leaving the gun behind, hoping I'd find it. Pinning this crime on me is logical.

Who'd believe a newcomer? And someone, most likely, without an alibi."

Ethan rested a comforting hand on my shoulder. "You're not alone. We know you didn't harm anyone. You're a victim in this mess."

I appreciated his words, but my temper simmered. "That's how I prove *my* innocence." I jabbed my finger toward the easel. "Before you say to leave this to the police, Amos is convinced I did it. You should have seen the look on his face when he found me holding the gun." I turned to Eddie. "And you had that same look—before you argue that he was doing his job. What happened to innocent until proven guilty?"

"Claudia, I'm sorry if I gave you the impression I jumped to a conclusion. My job is difficult at times, and we don't have a lot of unattended deaths in town. A couple per year, maybe. Most of those are accidents. I can't speak for Amos, but for me, I want to make sure we catch whoever is responsible. I didn't know Colton Prescott well, but had seen him in passing. He was a quiet man who kept to himself. He deserves justice."

"That's never been a question. Whoever harmed him needs to be held responsible. Do you jump to conclusions every time you investigate a crime?"

Ethan knelt on the floor next to me. "Claudia, put yourself in a police officer's shoes. There's a report of a gunshot. They go to investigate, find the door open, and you're near the body, holding a gun in your hands. What would you think?"

I didn't want to admit he made sense. "Eddie, you say you believe me. What can I do to help?"

"Nothing." He crossed to the window. "Out there is someone bold enough to break in here at least twice, attempt to frame you for murder, and lest we forget how this all started, Herman Grant died under mysterious circumstances. Ethan stated he was accustomed to using the inside stairs. After fifty years, he would have known every creak, but

Herman was found at the bottom, dead from blunt force trauma to the back of his head. It could have happened in a fall, but it's unlikely."

"Because it was the back of his head? Did the police label it suspicious and tell my grandmother the truth?"

Eddie said, "I spoke with your grandmother and relayed the accident's circumstances. When she asked if it would be safe for you to move to Drakes Bay, I informed her it was. There was no reason to think anyone would break in again."

"And now that someone has ransacked my great-uncle's room again and picked the lock to the shop, have you changed your mind?"

His chin dipped. "This was unexpected."

I snorted. "You do understatement well."

"If you and Beth want to be armchair sleuths, I have zero objections," he said. "But, going out and asking questions? That's another issue. You ladies need to remember, whoever this is won't hesitate to hurt you."

Beth's face paled for a fraction of an instant. "You don't have faith in us."

Eddie rubbed his hand over his chin. "You're not trained law enforcement. It's dangerous."

"I've listened to you and Dad talk about cases for years. I'm smart, and Claudia is perceptive. Didn't she realize Mr. X called her last night and *not* Prescott? Based on a vowel? That wasn't something you'd ever have discovered if it wasn't for her."

She had him on the fence now. He looked toward Ethan.

"Eddie's right. We don't want either of you to become the next target."

Herman's corporal form perched on the back of a chair. "Listen to them. Someone got the jump on me."

"I already am." I paced the apartment's width, pausing to stir the simmering marinara sauce.

Beth crossed her arms over her chest. "She's right. This

person will be back, and we need to be ready. Which means those cameras must be installed tonight." She pointed to the back door. "With both of you working on them, it'll be done in no time." Ethan nodded as he looked at Beth, her mouth set in a firm line and eyes narrowed.

"Beth's right. It's one action we can do to help."

Eddie followed his uncle out the door, and I heard their boots clomping on the stairs. "Thanks for sticking up for me."

"Are you kidding?" She grinned. "I love bossing them around. As the only girl in the family, it comes in handy, and I usually get my way." Her face grew somber. "They're right, you know. There's a target on your back. If something were to happen to you, all three cases would go cold. However, Prescott will be blamed for Herman's death, and you're blamed for Prescott's."

"There would still be what happened to me." A chill raced down my spine.

"If it were said you left town, no one would ever think differently. You could have an accident returning to the Big Apple."

I chewed my lower lip. "I don't like your train of thought. How would they keep you quiet? You'd know I didn't pack my bags and leave. I want to take up where Herman left off. Create beautiful clothes and be my own boss."

"We can talk over dinner." She turned on the water to fill the pasta pot.

I pondered the idea of disappearing like fog on a summer morning. "Even if you're right that someone might come after me, doesn't that make it crucial for us to find a way to outsmart the bad guys before they do?"

"If only we knew what Prescott was after."

Lola came trotting in with a tiny meow and paced in front of the pantry.

"Are you ready for dinner, little lady?" I opened the door and took out a can of seafood delight. Before I closed the door, I thought about that cubby hole in the floorboards. Could there be more evidence other than the cash box I overlooked in my excitement to find the date book?

"If Herman was careful about getting copies of the deed to the property, he must have discovered why Prescott wanted the building. I assume the two met, and it didn't go well."

"Why do you think they talked?"

"Mr. Prescott was confident when he called me. Almost like he had proof that Herman agreed to sell, and I didn't need to look through his papers."

"But I didn't." Herman zipped across the room, and a cool breeze wafted over me. At least I knew his ghostly form could move quickly when agitated. Not that it could do me much good.

Beth added a generous pinch of salt to the now-bubbling water. "I'll bet that's why the apartment was searched initially. That contract could prove to your family Herman agreed to sell."

"There was an agreement, and I remember tearing it up." Herman circled the room. "Someone should check the trashcans."

"Do you think the police took the garbage cans into evidence?"

"Hmm. We can ask Eddie and Dad; they'd know the standard procedure. What made you think Herman might have thrown something out?" She slid a pan of buttered bread into the oven.

"As your dad said, to think like Herman, and if there had been a meeting between him and Prescott, he was arrogant enough to hand Herman a contract. If that were me, I'd be ticked off, rip it up, and toss it."

"Excellent point. I like how you think. If they took the trash into evidence, it would still need to be at the station since the case remains unsolved." She gave me a high five. "Now we have something to investigate."

"No way anyone will let us look at the evidence." Once again, I chewed my lower lip. It was a bad habit I had when trying to figure out a problem.

"Maybe not, but what if we convince Eddie to take pictures?"

I brightened at the idea. "We can promise to keep mulling over ideas, and he can act on them."

Her shoulders sagged. "We'll miss all the fun."

I laughed softly. "I never said we wouldn't have our fingers crossed behind our backs when we say we'll stick to sofa sleuthing."

"I knew there was a reason we'd be friends." Putting a finger to her lips when we heard clomping on the steps, she winked. "We'll talk after they've left."

Eddie entered first. "Cameras are all set. Do you have your cell phone handy? We need to install the app and create an account."

I withdrew it from my pocket and handed it to him after I typed the passcode.

"You shouldn't be so trusting with your phone." He looked at the screen as he downloaded the app.

"If I can't trust the three people standing in my apartment, I might as well pack up and leave."

He handed me the phone. "Create a username; for heaven's sake, don't tell anyone your password."

"You're infuriating."

He grinned. "I'll take that as a compliment. When you're done, we'll walk through how to monitor them and set up alerts. You don't want to get an alarm for a squirrel or a leaf scuttling across the sidewalk."

It took three tries, but I selected a robust password that I could remember. Handing the phone back to Eddie, I said, "What's next?"

Beth interrupted as she pulled the bread from the oven. "Dinner. I don't want the pasta overcooked."

Ethan said, "I'm starved. The aroma of that garlic bread is making my mouth water."

"Psst, Claudia. There's an excellent merlot in the wine cellar. You should serve it to your guests."

I gave Herman a wink. "I'll be right back. Tonight is the first home-cooked meal from my kitchen. Even if I wasn't the chef, we deserve a nice bottle of red wine to go with it."

Eddie said, "I'll go with you."

I gave him a side eye. "As my personal bodyguard?"

"Until a few hours ago, you didn't know the wine cellar existed and you've been down those steep stairs once. I wouldn't want you to trip."

Beth said, "He has a point. Besides, he's an educated amateur when it comes to good wine. He'll select an excellent vintage."

I opened the door to the stairs and flicked the switch, but nothing happened. "It worked earlier, so maybe there's a faulty wire."

Eddie had his cell out, and his flashlight lit the treads. "Hold the handrail."

I groaned. "I know."

He laughed softly. "Gigi, you're going to liven things up around here."

I gave him a sharp glance, stumbled on the bottom step, and he grabbed my arm before I face-planted on the floor.

"Careful."

"What's with the Gigi?"

"For Grant's Gowns, and I think it suits you." His blue-gray eyes softened as my heart skipped a beat. "Do you mind?"

I shocked myself when I said, "I can get used to it."

He grinned. "Now, about that wine."

I crossed the room to the hidden panel, and the door eased open. As I flipped the switch, the light worked. A smile blossomed as I noticed the flashlight secured to the wall. "Thank you for this." I cautiously navigated the stairs, reaching the bottom without a mishap.

"This is a fantastic room." Eddie looked around, but his gaze wasn't casual. The hair pricked my arms.

"Is something wrong?"

He pressed a finger to his lips and made a circular motion with his hand. My feet seemed glued to the floor. Had someone been in here after we had left?

He prowled around the space, even the utility room, before he returned. "I think you should keep the basement door locked at all times—or at least until this situation is resolved." Taking my hand, he gave it a reassuring squeeze. "I'm not trying to frighten you, but I learned a long time ago to trust my instincts, and when we came down the steps, the vibe felt off."

"Maybe it's Herman's ghost?" My voice was a half octave higher.

His face relaxed. "I'm sure Herman moved on long ago. Be vigilant, okay?"

I nodded. Foolhardy wasn't my middle name. Eddie was cautioning me for some inexplicable reason. I trusted him with my life, and it wasn't because he was Beth's cousin. "I will."

"Good. Now, let's find a good wine and enjoy dinner. Beth's a fantastic cook. Ethan taught her everything he knows, and if you tell anyone this little secret, I'll deny it."

"Which is?" I cocked a brow and smiled.

"Beth should have been a chef. She'd be racking up Michelin stars with ease."

"That's high praise." I entered the wine room and felt the day's tension melt away.

"Gigi, I promise your taste buds will weep before dinner is over."

"I was down here earlier. Everything is safe." Herman

drifted between me and Eddie. "Is this young man flirting with you? I'm sure I could make him trip or something."

Eddie said, "If you don't mind, I'll just peruse the racks."

"Help yourself." I glared at Herman through narrowed eyes and pointed to the door.

He floated out as Eddie said, "This is an excellent collection. Call if you ever need a buddy to taste wine with you."

I wished Herman had heard Eddie refer to himself as a buddy. That was out of the flirting zone. "I'll keep that in mind."

After we came out, I firmly closed the door. "Beth and I were talking while you were outside. Do you know if the trashcan contents from the apartment and shop were taken as evidence?"

He clicked the light switch to the wine room off. "Why do you ask?"

"If Mr. Prescott had given Herman a contract to review, I'd bet he threw it out. It would be interesting to look at it."

"I don't like where you're headed."

I held up a hand. "You said we could mull over clues if we didn't act on them. What if you took the pictures so we could look at them? It might help resolve the question about a contract. Wouldn't that be worth checking out?"

We paused at the bottom of the stairs. If I could see inside Eddie's brain, I'd bet the wheels were churning. "Prescott implied there was a contract. Logically, it would be somewhere, with a duplicate copy in his office. Please say you'll see what you can find?"

"You have an interesting point. Prescott mentioned he had a contract for you to look at. I'm not saying I'll show you pictures of anything, but I will see what I find out. Will that suffice?"

I beamed, "For now," and ran up the steps.

11

Dinner was uneventful and, true to his word, Eddie showed me how to log in and check the cameras. I could save clips for up to a month and send them to someone.

"Put my number in your phone. Call or text if you need help, day or night." He rattled off the number. "Text me to make sure I have your number, too."

Beth watched our exchange with a smirk on her face as I tapped out a message to him.

His phone pinged with my text. "Good. I need to take off. Work tomorrow." He looked from me to Beth. "I trust you ladies will stay out of the investigation?"

I tried the innocent face I had used on my family members for years when I'd been up to no good. Hopefully, he'd buy it like they did. "My plans for tomorrow are to clean and organize the shop. Once cleared of the murder, I plan to open and, fingers crossed, get new customers."

Beth said, "Eddie, you'll check out the evidence taken from the apartment and shop after Herman's death?"

"Yes, and as I promised Claudia, I'll see if there was a contract at Prescott's."

Crossing my arms over my midsection, I thought, interesting, he didn't call me Gigi.

Ethan pushed back from the table. "I'll clean up."

I touched his forearm. "You will not. After you've installed locks and cameras, that's more than enough help."

He grinned. "For today, maybe." With a kiss on the top of Beth's head, he said, "I'm going to head out, too. Kiddo, you're staying here tonight?"

"Yes. I don't want Claudia to be alone. I might stay a few nights until Eddie and Amos get a better handle on what's happening. Despite having cameras, I wouldn't sleep well knowing she was here by herself."

Eddie nodded. "Not a bad idea." He gave me a steady look. "You have my number."

Beth covered her mouth with the back of her hand as her eyes twinkled. "Goodnight."

I walked Ethan and Eddie to the door. A dusting of snow had blown across the stairs. They walked down, single file, and when they reached the bottom, Ethan looked up and waved. "See you in the morning."

I turned to go inside when I froze in place. The treads on the stairs. "Beth, come quick."

Eddie and Ethan started up the steps. I held up my hand. "Wait there."

Beth poked her head out. What's going on?"

"Grab my phone. I left it on the table. And see if you can find a big flashlight."

Ethan said, "Is something wrong, Claudia?"

Breathless, I said, "Hold on. We might have a new clue."

Beth rushed out and handed me my phone and hers. "I'm sorry, but I couldn't find another flashlight. Use my cell."

What was it with Herman's lack of flashlights? I bent low and pulled up the pictures I had taken earlier of the boot tread we discovered near the shop door. "I'm not an expert, but your and Eddie's boot prints look identical to those outside the back door from whoever broke in. Look at these pictures."

Beth peered over my shoulder and studied the new footprints Ethan and Eddie made. With a low whistle, she said, "You gotta see this."

I took a few new pictures so that we could compare.

Eddie ran up the stairs and held out his hand. I handed him my phone. Ethan was next to him, and he looked at the images from earlier and their footprints. "This isn't great news. Most people around here have these winter work boots: construction workers, firemen, police, road crew, and some women, too. The tread is deep and provides excellent traction."

"Can you tell if it's a man's or woman's boot?"

He shook his head. "They're unisex. The best we can try to determine is the size. Do you mind if I send your pictures from this morning and the shots of our prints to my phone for comparison?"

I took my phone and then sent the images to Eddie and Ethan.

Quietly, he said, "I saw what you did there, Gigi."

Beth said, "Documentation is not the pursuit of the truth."

Ethan groaned. "Eddie, let's table this for tonight." He pointed to the door. "Go inside and lock up. If you get scared later, call one or both of us."

I wrapped my arms around my waist. "Thanks, and I appreciate you."

After Beth and I went inside, I locked the door and sagged against the jamb. "I had hoped the boots would be unique."

"Unless a person purchases online, we all shop from the same few stores or drive to Freeport for outlet shopping."

I marched into the kitchen. "Ice cream?" I chuckled when I saw a sour expression on her face. "Not the remnants from Herman; I bought a few pints today."

"Let me load the dishwasher while you do that, and then we can study the board again. There has to be something we're overlooking."

"Suspects and motive." I scooped vanilla raspberry swirl into deep bowls and added a maple cookie for crunch. "Currently, the only people who've popped up are the troublesome trio."

Closing the dishwasher door, Beth pushed the start button and took the bowls from me. "I've known them all my life. To think one of them killed Herman and Prescott?" She shook her head. "Doubtful."

"They showed up at his place right after the cops. Also, they were close enough to say they heard the gunshot. It's always this way in the movies—the murderer lurks around the edge but is not a likely suspect."

We settled into our respective cushions as our spoons clinked against the bowls. From time to time, I glanced at the board. I got up and added the women's names in the Prescott column. At least now there was more information. "Did you see anyone else while we sat in the Jeep, and I mustered the courage to knock on the door?"

She closed her eyes. "Give me a minute."

I wasn't going to rush her. We had plenty of time to dissect every nuance of the morning. Had I only discovered a dead man, accused of murder, had someone break into my new home again, and ordered me to the police station for questioning in the morning? We had all night to dissect the details. I'd be prepared for Amos and Eddie's interrogation.

"The only person we saw, well, vehicle, was that dark pickup that roared past us as we drove down the street."

I bobbed my finger. "Right." I got up and added that to the board in the Prescott column. "One of the women insinuated that she liked shopping at Grant's Gowns. Is it possible one of them quarreled with Herman, and it got out of hand?" I glanced around the room. Where was my ghostly uncle when I needed him to overhear our conversation?

"Couldn't the two incidents be separate?"

I set my now-empty bowl aside. "Do you believe in coincidence?"

She munched her cookie. "Not typically, but it's in the realm of possibility."

"I get that you don't want to think your former classmates might have committed a senseless crime. But anyone can snap when pushed too far."

Lola sauntered into the room from the hallway, flicking her tail. A cobweb suitable for a haunted house clung to it. "Where have you been snooping?"

She hopped up and purred. Running my hand over her fluffy tail, I said, "Have you been searching for clues?"

Herman floated in. "She was under my bed. Sorry to say I rarely dusted under there, but she was curled up on top of a box I had forgotten about. It's worth looking at."

I set her down. "Since I just said there is no such thing as coincidence, I'm going to see where she found the dust bunny bigger than her." I knew under my bed it was clear, but I started there. Beth couldn't read my mind and know it came from Herman's room. I also didn't want to freak her out since it would be her room for the night.

The bedroom doors were open, and I pulled the shades in my room before flicking on the overhead light. I searched the corners, got down on my hands and knees, and peered under the bed.

"Anything?"

"No, just my suitcase." I stood and brushed my hands on my yoga pants. "The closet doors are closed, so she wasn't in there." For Beth's benefit, I did a cursory scan of the bathroom, but that was spotless.

Next, I closed the shades in Herman's former room and turned on the bedside table lamps. A soft, warm glow filled the room. "I can see why Herman liked this space; it's cozy." I dropped to my knees, and Beth did the same on the opposite side. "Lots of dust. I'll need to get the mop under here tomorrow. What's that?" I slid on my belly and pushed a small box toward Beth. "Wait a sec. There's a wad of paper under a leg at the head of the bed. Could it just be holding up a wobbly post?"

Pushing the box aside, she said, "Can you reach it?"

"Ugh." I tried, and groaned. "It's wedged and I can't without tearing it."

"Hold on. I'll lift the bed. You can slide it out. Wait until I say I've firmly got the bed. I don't want it crashing on your fingers." She stepped over me. "One more minute."

I sneezed. That dust mop would come in handy as soon as I got off the floor.

"Ready?"

"Yup." My hand hovered over the edge of the paper, waiting for enough space to free it without nary a tear.

"Go for it."

The bed was steady as I eased the wad to me. "Got it."

Beth said, "I'm setting the bed into place as soon as you're out."

The extra wiggle room was helpful. I slid over the floor and sat up. Dust covered the front of my top. I held up the paper and box. "Who's ready for sofa sleuthing?"

"That might be our new favorite phrase." She pulled me up from the floor.

I cringed and sneezed again. I handed her the box and paper, and with a laugh, I said, "No peeking. It's not Christmas."

"You might want to change your top. I'll wait for you in the living room."

After a quick change, I retrieved the dust mop and ran it under the bed and around the room. Herman drifted in and watched as I tidied up a bit more.

I whispered, "Don't spook Beth while she's sleeping."

"It never crossed my mind. All I wanted to say is I'm glad she's staying. You've had a couple of emotionally taxing days, and having a friend around would be nice."

That was an understatement. "Hopefully, it'll get better."

"Did you mention that you'll work in the shop tomorrow?"

I leaned on the mop handle. "I can't wait to deep clean and do inventory. Then I'll need to service the sewing machines and design a few ready-to-wear dresses for the spring season."

His chin dropped. "Sundresses are popular for summer. Vacationers often dropped by to pick up something special. Have you thought of a label?"

Could a ghost be melancholy? "I have. The existing label is perfect. I'm going to add *by Claudia* to it. Herman, I don't want to erase all you've accomplished. I plan on growing the business from a solid foundation."

Beth called out, "Are you okay in there?"

"I'll be right out, just talking to the dust bunnies." I cringed. That sounded super lame. I wished I could give Herman a comforting hug. "We'll talk about the shop when we're alone."

"You've made this old ghost very happy."

The box and paper were next to Lola, and Beth held a marker. "I'm dying of curiosity."

"Sorry for the delay. Once I saw the floor under the bed, I had to run the mop over it." I sat down and picked up the box, shaking it. "It doesn't rattle."

She popped her hand on her hip. "It's not a puppy."

"Good thing, or I would have made it dizzy." I eased off the top and folded back the tissue paper. Nestled in the center was a blue velvet bag. I tugged the cords and turned it upside down. A corkscrew fell into my palm. I laughed. "Herman must have received this as a gift or was giving it and didn't get the chance."

"My guess is he was giving it. I store presents under my bed all the time."

"Me, too." I held the folded paper as my heart rate kicked up. "This has to be a clue."

"Open it." She perched on the sofa's edge, picking up and setting Lola in her lap.

I carefully unfolded the small square because I wasn't sure how easily the paper might tear. The first two folds revealed a piece of delicate tissue paper used to make patterns. I continued taking care not to rip it. Surely, he hadn't regularly used this type of paper in his sewing? I preferred sturdy Kraft paper when I created a pattern.

"What does it say."

I placed the box top on my lap, smoothed the paper over it, and scanned the page. "It's a series of numbers: 7, 75, 43, 82."

"That must be a combination for a safe. Or a passcode to a bank account."

I looked up. "Or meaningless." Herman was hovering over my shoulder.

"Herman never struck me as the type to keep something that had no meaning."

"Alright, let's assume it's the combination for a safe."

"He camouflaged the access to the basement, so it has to be down there." She snapped her fingers. "I'll bet you find it when you clean the store. But why leave the numbers in plain sight?"

"They're useless unless you know where the safe is and I found one."

Her mouth dropped open. "Cool. Should we try the numbers?"

"Not tonight." I wasn't sure why I was hesitating, but Herman nodded.

"I wouldn't have left clues in the safe."

Beth said, "If anyone had discovered the scrap of paper, they would have figured it was nothing."

I folded the paper and placed it in the box. "Exactly. But if it turns out to be the combination, it was very clever of my uncle to tuck it there. At first glance, it was steadying the headboard. Hiding something in plain sight is the best way to throw up a smoke screen."

12

____

After a restless night, I tiptoed past Beth's door and padded down the hall. The floors were ice cold against my bare feet. Lola sprawled across the kitchen table. I scooped her up, kissed between her ears, and said, "Naughty girl, on the table." I placed her on the floor. "Coffee first, then breakfast for all." I measured coffee and water and hit the button. Next up, get dressed.

She wound around my legs, warming my ankles. "You're a flirty little fur ball this morning."

"Excuse me. Claudia?" Herman appeared at the counter. "Would you mind if I stayed with you in the shop? I want to explain everything while you organize."

"That's fine, but if anyone pops in like Beth or Ethan, you'll have to float or whatever we should call it."

"And will you tell me what happens at the police station? You might learn a tidbit to help me remember how I ended up like this." He ran a translucent hand down his form.

I glanced down the hall.

"Don't worry, we're alone. Beth left thirty minutes ago."

"She did?" I wasn't sure why I felt disappointed. "Then breakfast for one." I hurried down the hall to get ready. Since

I had to answer questions, I wore comfortable clothes: a dark turtleneck sweater, jeans, and thick socks. I'd be warm, if nothing else, to avoid fidgeting in the chair. Confidence was key in this type of situation, right?

A tapping on the glass door had me call out, "Coming."

Beth waved when she saw me. I pulled open the door. "What are you doing out there?"

She held a white paper bag and stamped the snow off her boots onto the rug. "When I checked the kitchen for breakfast items, I saw you bought eggs and chicken breakfast sausage, but nothing sweet to balance the healthy stuff. I zipped down to Brewed Bliss and picked up some treats. Apple fritters were the only logical choice since there's fruit, covering three food groups."

I took the bag. "Come in. I just put coffee on and was going to feed Lola." Looking over my shoulder, she hung up her coat and kicked off her boots. Today, she wore a long mauve sweater coat, a cream turtleneck, and black velvet slacks.

"You look nice. Did you make that sweater?"

"Thanks. Yeah, I made the sweater a few years ago. It'll keep me warm when we're at the station."

"You're coming with me?" I placed the bag next to the stove.

"I have to give a statement, and if you think I'm going to leave you there without support, what kind of sidekick would I be?"

A cold shiver raced down my spine. "Do you think I need a lawyer?"

"You're not under arrest, but I'll text Dad for his advice." She pulled the phone from her sweater pocket and tapped the screen while I filled Lola's bowls with fresh water and food. Then, I placed a skillet on the stovetop.

"Scrambled, fried, over easy, or sunny side up?"

She frowned. "Dad reminded me he'll meet us here at nine and we can go over together."

"Why the face?"

"Huh?" She looked up. "Nothing. Dad's never been a fan of Amos Branson. He treats everyone like a criminal, including other police officers. Dad doesn't want us to deal with him alone."

"Even Ethan and Eddie? Sounds like he's insecure."

"Amos attempts to intimidate them, but they refuse to accept it. Have you heard of cops who swagger around thinking they're hotshots? That's Amos. He expected to be promoted to chief when Dad retired."

"I didn't realize your dad had been head of the department."

"Yeah, he doesn't talk about it. When he left, they hired Dave Durgin. He's fair and a good cop. I'm sure you'll meet him today since he likes to stay informed about everything happening in town."

I pressed a hand to my flipping tummy. "Should I be nervous?" It might be silly to ask the question since I already was.

Her face brightened. "Not in the least. This is all routine, and the evidence proves you had nothing to do with the shooting."

"Except no one can give me an alibi for the time when Prescott was most likely shot."

"No," she drawled. "Look at it from a different viewpoint. No one can put you or your Jeep on Ocean View before yesterday morning. I know it's hard, but try not to worry. Walking through the door nervous will only make things worse."

That was true. "We should ask Eddie about the phone call that reported the gunshot. There must be caller ID at the station, and don't they log all calls?"

She smacked the table. "How could we have overlooked that question yesterday?"

"Shock, disbelief, and feeling overwhelmed are just a few words that spring to mind." I poured two mugs of coffee. Herman remained quiet, for which I was grateful. I handed her the carton of creamer and nudged the sugar bowl over before I sat down.

"Beth, I'm scared."

She placed her hand over mine and tipped her head. "It's understandable. We should be out of the station by ten. Shortly after that, you'll be up to your elbows in hot water and suds, and I'll be waiting for customers ready to shop."

"I will never be able to repay you for your kindness. You've gone above and beyond for someone you just met."

"Are you kidding? I haven't had this much excitement in forever."

Forcing a smile, I asked, "So, about those eggs?"

*E*than opened the steel door to the police station, and Beth and I followed him inside. As we took our first few steps into the lobby, an oppressive weight settled on my shoulders. I looked at my feet to see if they had sunk into the floor. Amos awaited us, his hands resting on his holster and his chest puffed out.

"Ethan, I'm surprised to see you. This is just routine questioning." He gave me a sharp glare.

"I have no doubt. You understand this was shocking for the girls to discover Colton Prescott. I wanted to be here to provide support. Are you also interviewing Kasey Pelham, Barbara Hall, and Julie Clinton? They arrived on the scene fairly quickly after you."

His eyes narrowed. "Are you trying to tell me how to do my job?" I heard a distinct by mild growl in Amos's voice.

I glanced at Beth, who watched her father.

"We both know how to do your job. Today, I'm here as a concerned father and friend."

If Amos hadn't been so quick to label me a killer, I wouldn't have needed Ethan's support. After seeing the officer again, I was grateful that Ethan was with us.

"Officer Branson, has there been any progress on the break-in at my place yesterday?"

He blinked hard. "I'm sure it was kids or a petty thief case. Nothing to be alarmed about. But we haven't closed the case, if it eases your mind."

"Excuse me if I'm wrong, but I thought cases remained open until they were solved."

"In situations like this, we may never know who was responsible. I attribute it to a crime of opportunity. The shop had been empty for months. If someone had been watching the place and noticed the lights on, they likely decided to see if they could grab some quick cash. Once you left, it provided them the perfect chance to take a few things."

That didn't make a bit of sense. My things remained untouched. If someone were looking for cash or jewelry, of which I had neither, they would have searched my room, not simply shoved the clothes and shoes around in my closet. Herman's belongings were the target. Why was he deflecting? Unless he believed I killed Mr. Prescott and intended on wrapping up his case today. My knees weakened, and I stumbled back against the wall.

Beth took my arm. "What's wrong?"

"It's nothing." I couldn't tell her what I thought with Amos staring at me. I locked my knees, looked him in the eye. "I'm ready if you are."

"Follow me." He gave a curt nod to Ethan. "If you must, you can sit in on the interviews, but you can't ask or answer any questions."

"Can Beth join us?" She was holding my arm which was keeping me upright, and I was grateful. Projecting confidence was one thing, but my body resisted the idea completely. My knees felt weak, and my stomach churned. I regretted eating a large breakfast.

"For this first round, yes. If I must question you again, it will just be you and me."

A cold sweat gripped me. I wanted to protest. Ethan caught my eye and blinked slowly. I took it as a sign not to say anything

Amos stood in the doorway to a room with a long metal table, two black plastic chairs on each side, one wall with a full-width mirror, and a camera in the upper left corner. This was an interrogation room. I attempted to swallow the lump in my throat, but it wouldn't budge.

"Take a seat." He pointed to the chairs on the right.

I pulled out the first one for Beth. I took the one closer to the wall. With any luck, it'd open and swallow me. Ethan sat on the other side. After Amos closed the door with a firm *thud,* he took the seat diagonally from me.

He glanced over his shoulder at the camera and gave a satisfied smirk. Was this a tactic to ratchet up my nerves? It was working.

He placed a notebook on the table, opened it to a blank page, and wrote the date and time before looking at me. "Ms. Grant, I'd like for you to review the events leading up to your arrival and the subsequent discovery you made inside 26 Ocean View, the home of Colton Prescott."

"Should I start when I received the first phone call from Mr. Prescott?"

He cocked a brow. "Had you been in contact with him before that call?"

I shook my head. "No. I had only arrived in Drakes Bay that morning. Beth and Ethan were at my apartment when he called. Ethan recorded the call."

"That was three days ago, and I know about the recorded

call. It's evidence that's not admissible in court." He wrote something down that I couldn't read. "Continue."

His tone set my teeth on edge. "Mr. Prescott requested a meeting at ten o'clock, and I agreed."

"Why would you agree to meet a man you didn't know alone at his home?" His calm gaze never wavered.

"Mr. Prescott said that he'd been in negotiations with Herman for the sale of the dress shop and that he'd sweeten the deal by twenty-five percent for my inconvenience of relocating to Maine."

"You were interested in selling something you had just inherited?"

I leaned forward. "I didn't know about the inheritance until Ethan told me. I thought my grandmother was Herman's beneficiary. She encouraged me to reopen the dress shop even though Herman had passed."

"Why wouldn't she have told you the truth? Was she afraid you'd be out for some quick cash so you wouldn't have to work?"

"You'd need to ask her. I can provide her phone number if you'd like, but she knew it was my dream to own a shop. I believe this was her encouraging me to act on it."

"I have her number on file. Why did you agree to meet with the victim if you weren't interested in selling?"

This conversation was an interrogation. I wanted to ask why he was treating me like a criminal, but I kept quiet. "Curiosity? Ethan told me about Mr. Prescott's attempt to purchase the store before Herman died, and he reassured me that wasn't something Herman wanted. He looked forward to me moving to town and working with him as his apprentice."

He cleared his throat. "Ethan, you seem to have a vested interest in these events."

"There's nothing wrong with Claudia having the facts. Besides, I didn't want her going alone, so Beth accompanied her. Which, in hindsight, I should have gone, too."

"Prescott was already dead, and Ms. Grant doesn't have an alibi for the time of death."

Placing my hands palms down on the table, I looked him in the eyes. "Officer Branson, I did not kill Colton Prescott. I swear, I'm telling the truth."

"Then why did I find you holding the gun used to murder Prescott? Did you forget it the night before when you shot him? Did you think you could use Beth as an alibi when you went back to get it?"

"No." My heart hammered in my chest.

"Prove where you were between ten p.m. and eight a.m. yesterday morning."

"Is that the time frame in which you believe Mr. Prescott was killed?"

He snapped. "Ms. Grant, I'm not here to answer your questions. Tell me, can anyone vouch for you?"

Beth said, "I can. She was home all night."

I swiveled in my chair. "Beth?"

"Last year, Dad installed exterior cameras on the front of my store. One exposure captures Grant's Gowns and the parking area where Claudia's Jeep is parked."

Ethan said, "We can get you access."

"Why are you divulging this information now?"

Beth narrowed her eyes, and color flushed her cheeks a deep red. "I've sat here and listened as you've tried to mold facts to fit the narrative you've created. You'd better acknowledge Claudia's innocence and stop attempting to pin this crime on her. It wasn't some kid or petty criminal who broke into her building. You don't want to accept that a local person could have committed these crimes. I, for one, believe the same person who broke into her store the minute she left had already killed Prescott and called in the gunshot, after giving her enough time to reach Ocean View, thus framing her."

Amos crossed his arms over his chest and leaned back in

his chair. "Quite the speech from someone who doesn't know what kind of person Ms. Grant is, don't you think, Beth?"

"See for yourself. Look at the footage. You can't deny facts. She never left the building."

"She could have walked." His expression was smug. "And what would you say if I told you an eyewitness saw a woman entering Prescott's house around eleven?"

"That doesn't prove it was Claudia, and if you had proof, why haven't you arrested her?"

A flick of anger flashed in his eyes. This was a cop who didn't like to be challenged.

Ethan stood. "You're finished fishing, Amos. Either tell me who your witness is and bring them in for questioning, or we're leaving."

"You don't have the right to tell me what to do." Amos didn't bother to stand but leaned forward and shook his finger at Beth and me. "Get out of here but, Ms. Grant, do yourself a favor and don't leave town. Better yet, don't leave your store. I wouldn't want anyone saying they saw you so much as jaywalking. I might be forced to slap handcuffs on you."

Ethan signaled toward the door. "Girls."

We hurried ahead of him, but I slowed my steps to hear what Ethan might say to Amos.

"Back off. I'm no longer your superior, but you're chasing the wrong lead. Herman's attack and Prescott's murder are linked, just like whoever broke into Claudia's residence. Do your job, Amos."

Amos's tone was low and menacing. "I follow the evidence just as you taught me. Now leave my police station." He caught me watching them. "Ms. Grant, you might want to consider hiring a lawyer. Just in case."

13

———

How I managed to get into the car and return to my apartment remains a mystery. Beth wrapped her arms around me as we sat on the sofa.

Ethan handed me a mug of steaming tea and knelt in front of me. "He's all bluff and has no follow-through, so try not to worry. I'm sure it's hard, but you've got Eddie, Beth, and me in your corner. We know you're innocent."

"Am I overreacting, or does it seem he doesn't care about the truth? All he wants to do is lock me up, to solve his problem."

Beth glanced at her dad. "We won't let that happen. Dad, we should find Claudia a lawyer. Just in case."

He nodded. "I have someone from Portland in mind." He patted my hand. "I'll call him if that's okay with you, Claudia?"

I nodded and squeezed my eyes shut to fight back tears. "This is a nightmare. I wish I'd never gone to see that man." Opening my eyes, I said, "Who do you think the person was who came forward to say they saw a woman going into Prescott's?"

"I suspect one of the troublesome trio. They live on Ocean

View and act as a self-appointed neighborhood watch when it suits them. Wait." Beth approached the board, took a picture of our notes, and then erased them. She drew what looked like a street with various large X's on either side of the lines. She placed a capital P, and I understood where she was heading.

For the first time since leaving the police station, I smiled. "We need a paper flip chart."

"That wouldn't hurt." She added in circles. "Trees are all over that neighborhood, which would keep neighbors from spying on neighbors."

"You're trying to determine which house had a clear line of sight to the front of his house."

"Right." She jabbed the marker in my direction. "Remember, you parked beside the walkway leading to the front door. With all those trees and shrubs, the house is obscured."

I jumped up and did a jig. "Which means no one could have seen anyone enter or exit the home unless they were standing on the street looking directly at the front door. Either the woman is lying or"

Ethan said, "There is no woman." He slammed his fist into his open hand. "That jerk. He's trying to create a scenario where you'd feel backed into a corner and confess to something you didn't do. Not to worry. I'll speak to the chief."

"Ethan, please don't. At least not yet. I'm sure it's just his way of trying to solve the case. He does have a point. No one in town knows my background, and I'm a stranger. I showed up, and Prescott's life ended."

Herman floated into the room. "What's happened? You look paler than a ghost." He chuckled. "I made a paranormal joke."

I shook my head at Herman's lame attempt at levity. Beth crossed the room and hugged me.

"Claudia, we're good judges of character." She tapped the

middle of her chest. "I know you're innocent, and Dad does, too."

"Thank you. Your support means a lot." I studied the board again. "Where do each of the women live? Could they have seen a car or truck on the street? Also, do we know if a male or female reported the sound of a gunshot?"

Ethan asked, "Do you think it's relevant to proving your innocence to Amos?"

"The same person who said they saw a person enter Prescott's probably called in the gunshot right after we arrived. That could have been the person who killed him, and I'm a convenient fall girl."

"An excellent scenario and certainly plausible," Beth said as she withdrew her phone. "I'm going to text Eddie to see if he can gather any details on the witness report regarding a woman entering the home and remind him about researching the evidence we've discussed."

I remained quiet while she typed. Herman studied the board. "I can give you an alibi for the night Prescott was killed. I was here all night, and ghosts never sleep."

I appreciated his offer; however, it wouldn't be helpful since I was the only living person aware that a ghost was even present.

A soft whoosh sound indicated Beth's text was off in cyberspace. "Will you be all right if I go to my store?"

"Beth, I'm fine. You heard Amos; he said I should stay home, which was my plan. I have a full day to clean the store, complete my inventory, and check the computer system. As long as I'm not incarcerated, I'd like to open for business next month."

Ethan gave a brisk nod. "That's an excellent idea. We're just a phone call away."

Beth said, "Or text. Want to have dinner tonight?"

As much as I'd like to say yes, I declined. "I'm sure I'll be exhausted. A hot bath, reheating some pasta, and binge-watching Netflix will be the most I can manage after a long day."

She gave me a close look. "If you change your mind, I can be here in five minutes."

"Much appreciated. Go do knitting things." I forced a bright smile that I hoped was convincing and walked them to the back door.

Ethan paused, his hand hovering over the doorknob. "Keep the cameras on. Do you know how to check them and take clips if necessary?"

"Eddie made sure I was comfortable with the software, and he set my cell phone to ping if they went off. I can check all views at any time."

Beth bit her lower lip. "Are you sure you don't want me to hang around? I'm a great organizer, and you know I'm a whiz with a cleaning rag."

I smiled at her. "You've done more than enough."

Ethan opened the door. A blast of cold air wafted into the room. I shivered.

Beth said, "We'll leave, but I'll call you later. If you don't answer the phone, I'm showing up."

I chuckled. "Yes, ma'am."

She wrapped her scarf around her neck and followed Ethan down the stairs. I waited at the top until they safely reached the bottom. A few snowy steps still lay covered where the sun hadn't yet reached. She turned to wave.

I returned the gesture. "Talk to you later."

*A*fter they walked out of view, I went into the kitchen to brew a fresh pot of coffee. Lola slinked into the room, gave a tiny meow, and hopped onto the chair. Herman perched on the table.

"I know it makes zero difference to you but, Herman, could you sit on a chair and not the table?"

"Sorry, I've been rattling around this place long before you arrived. I got into some bad habits. I'll change them."

"Thank you."

"For what it's worth, you'll truly enjoy being a shop owner once all this Prescott nonsense is behind you. Collaborating with customers to select fabrics, designing the perfect outfit for any occasion, and offering ready-to-wear options are excellent sellers."

"Who was your typical client?"

"Anyone who loved pretty and flattering clothes. There were custom designs for wedding gowns, but day dresses and outfits were an excellent source of revenue. My favorite part of the job was working with brides." He sighed. "Being a small part of a woman's special day filled me with pride. Knowing they trusted me to help them shine was an honor."

"Did you design many gowns each year?"

"Approximately fifteen were originals. The bride would often come in asking to have her mother's dress remade, which was a challenging task, but I loved the entire process. When they start flocking to your door, you'll see what I mean."

My face fell. "If I'm successfully framed for murder, that won't ever happen."

"Trust Ethan. He won't let an innocent person go to jail. Amos thinks highly of himself and is a class-A jerk but still a decent cop. It would tarnish his reputation if he didn't get the guilty party."

"You keep saying that, but why is your case still unsolved if that's true?" The coffee pot gurgled to a finish, and I poured myself a cup. Leaning against the counter, I took a mind-clearing sip.

"It's tied to what happened to Prescott. I've started to think about everything that happened before I," he coughed, "died. I'm convinced Prescott didn't kill me."

"Why?" I sat, relieved to have time to talk openly with Herman.

"He wanted the property. As a smart businessman, he would have found a way to convince me to sell. Either offer more money or sweeten the deal in other ways. He was prepared to offer you more money."

"I'm not certain about that. Without the original contract and the one he was supposed to provide me, there's no way to determine if he was telling the truth."

"He didn't know that you weren't aware of the specifics. I guess he planned on making you an offer that would be impossible to refuse. There's nothing special about this place except the location. The view of the bay is priceless. The shop could be converted into a restaurant and be more profitable than selling dresses, and the rent on this apartment could be astronomical."

Those were excellent points. I finished my mug of coffee. "I'm going to put on sneakers, peek in your cubby, and then we'll change that light bulb on the stairs. It's time to get things shipshape."

Herman's ghostly form rose. "What can I do to help?"

It was comical that a ghost was offering to help me. "Keep me company? If anyone were to wander by and hear me talking, they'll think I'm a person who talks to myself."

"Turn a radio on. It will drown out your voice if anyone lingers."

"You're a fountain of good ideas. I wish I could hug you."

The corners of his mouth drooped. "Knowing you want to is enough."

I offered him a sad smile. "Once we solve your murder, you'll be able to cross over. During the last couple of days, I've gotten accustomed to you popping up."

"I'll be leaving my shop and home in capable hands." With a gentle wave of his hand, he gestured toward the hall.

"Sneakers, you have work to do. Lola and I are excellent supervisors."

I opened the pantry door and pushed the bottles aside. Prying up the floorboard for the second time I stuck my hand in the opening. My fingers grazed a small book. I pulled out the cash box and Herman's passport. I chuckled. "That's not going to solve this case."

"Mad money's in the box. It's yours now, spend as you wish." Herman said, "One mystery solved. We'll meet you downstairs."

I returned both items to the cubby and closed the lid.

*P*erched on the ladder, I had just screwed in the lightbulb. The stairs flooded with light. Other than dust and stacks of boxes on the edge of each stair, they were in good shape. Herman tripping and falling to his death was unlikely, but still possible. A glint of something halfway down caught my eye. I descended the ladder and pushed it against the kitchen wall. Hurrying down the steps, I picked up one half of a four-leaf clover with the words *hope* and *love* embossed into the leaves.

I ran down the stairs, calling to Herman. "Can you come here for a minute? I've found something, and it could be a clue."

"Here I am, Gigi."

I chuckled. "Et tu, dear uncle?"

"It was a hoot when Eddie called you that. I like it. Now," rubbing his ghostly hands together, he said, "what can I help with?'

"Is this your good luck charm?"

"It would be very unlucky to have just one half, but will you turn it over so I can see both sides?"

I did, and he frowned. "I don't recall ever seeing that. I

wasn't a fan of lucky talismans. I believe people create their good fortune."

"It was on the stairs, about halfway up."

He floated to the open doorway. "No one ever took them except for Lola and me." He twirled around. "This has to belong to the killer or the person who snuck in here yesterday."

Now, I wish I hadn't picked it up without using a tissue. Once again, I tainted a vital piece of evidence. "I don't remember seeing it before. It had to have been dropped yesterday."

"When Eddie calls you later or maybe stops by, you can show it to him." He tried to nudge my arm, but his arm slipped through mine.

"Herman," I glanced down and gave him a playful warning, "that's another thing that is a little weird."

"Got it. It's too bad I was in the attic when whoever it was broke in."

More new information. "We have an attic? Why didn't you tell me that before? There could be important clues just waiting to be discovered. Will you show me?"

"That won't happen unless you have someone with you. There are low beams and a rickety access ladder, and, might I remind you, if you got stuck up there, no one would know."

I stamped my foot as frustration built. He was right, but I wasn't going to tell him that. "Fine. I'll have Beth come over, and we can check it out. How will I tell her I know about the space?"

"Go out the back door to your Jeep and look up. You'll see the windows. While you're up there, check out the view. If you ever wanted to build up, say you had a family, there's plenty of space for more bedrooms, and the view is magnificent."

"In the foreseeable future, I'm swamped. Staying out of jail and building a business requires a twenty-four-seven commitment. There's no time for a construction project or for finding a partner to have a baby with."

"What if a handsome police officer asked you out for dinner? Or some other nice local person. You'd need to go to be polite, and you never know what might happen while you're hard at work." Herman floated to the front of the store. "Claudia, you should come out here. Someone is trying to peer in the window."

I stashed the charm in my jeans pocket, ran my hand through my hair, and hurried out front. Amos. I turned the lock before opening the door. He filled the doorway.

"Ms. Grant, I decided to drop by to make sure you had taken my advice." He squinted as he looked over my shoulder. "Are you alone?"

14

***

Stammering, I said, "No, yes. Well, just for a minute. Beth had to run across the street, but she'll be right back." I hated lying, but the glint in Amos's eyes made the hair on the back of my neck stand up.

"Since you're by yourself, maybe I should look around to ensure your safety." He stepped forward. I had to open the door wider to allow him to enter. I glanced toward Knit or Purl, wishing I had a way to signal Beth.

Herman appeared next to me. "You'll be okay. I'm here."

A ghost telling me I would be fine didn't erase my fears. I closed the door and flicked on the outside lights. If Beth happened to look out her door, she might think it was odd and pop over. If he tried to arrest me, I'd get one phone call, and she would be that person.

"How can I help you, Officer?"

His gaze scanned the room. "You've got some cleaning to do before you can open."

"Yes, and inventory, too. I'm looking forward to getting the shop settled and sewing again." I tucked my hands into my jeans pockets; my fingertips grazed the partial four-leaf clover. "Does the lady in your life prefer dresses or slacks?"

"At the moment, no wife or girlfriend." His fixed his gaze on my face. "Would you like to make a play for a handsome police officer?"

I shook my head, "Thanks, but I'm happily single. Starting a business isn't for the faint of heart, and I don't expect to have much time to date, let alone fall in love and be in a committed relationship."

"Smart girl. I like that." He gave me a wink. "If you change your mind, give me a call." He crossed the room to the dressing area and pushed open each door to the private rooms. "Herman did a good business. Too bad about what happened. Nice old guy."

I felt a cool breeze across my cheek and knew Herman was close. "Did you know my uncle well?"

"We met regularly to chat. Like I'm sure we'll do eventually. It's good for people to see the police have a presence in the businesses around town. It keeps everyone safe, and the proprietors sleep better at night, knowing we have a close eye on what's happening."

With a nod and forced smile, I said, "A strong police force is always appreciated."

"I'm glad we're on the same page." He gave me a pointed look that I couldn't interpret. "No trouble last night?"

"All was as quiet as a church." I wiggled my fingers behind my back, trying to ease the tension that cramped them.

He withdrew a business card from his chest pocket. "If you need anything, day or night, you don't need to call 9-1-1, call me. I'll come right over. This way, if you had a prowler or something, it wouldn't go out over the radio where the perp might be tuned in and know help was on the way. The element of surprise is always best."

I took the card and saw a ten-digit number.

"My personal cell number." He gave a brisk nod. "I did the same for your uncle, and he never had a bit of trouble."

"Thank you, Officer Branson."

"You can call me Amos. The only people who use the formalities are the elderly and newbies. I have a feeling you'll be around a long time."

"Does this mean you no longer think I'm responsible for Mr. Prescott's death?" This was a strange twist.

"The evidence points toward your innocence, but we shall see how it goes." He strode past me and paused with his hand on the knob. "Take care, Claudia. I'll be seeing you." He closed the door with a *thud*.

I stared after him. "That has to be the oddest conversation since I arrived. He's like two sides of a coin." My cell rang.

"Hey, Beth." I smiled.

"Hi. Is everything okay over there? I see your outside light is on, and Amos just left. Was he harassing you?"

"He stopped in to see how I was, and we had the strangest conversation. He gave me his personal cell and said to call day or night if I needed anything. It was better than calling 9-1-1. And that's not all. He indicated he and Herman were chummy."

"Really? That is odd. Amos doesn't chat up anyone without a specific purpose."

"He said that providing shop owners in town with peace of mind knowing their police force was always on standby, should be comforting. But it was more about contacting him directly. If I had an issue, I wouldn't call him. He gives me the willies."

Beth laughed, easing my discomfort. "Was there anything about the conversation that didn't?"

"Nope, he even said to think of him when I was ready to start dating."

She gasped. "Don't tell me you're considering going out with him?"

I laughed and looked out my front window at her shop. "Not in this lifetime." Growing serious, I said, "Hey, if you see my outside light on during the day can we use that as a signal that I might need help? At least until this murder is resolved. Being new in town, I don't know who to trust except you, Ethan, and Eddie. Everyone is a stranger."

"Of course, and I'll let Dad know, too. Might not be bad to tell Eddie since he patrols town as part of his route."

"Good idea. If you see him, feel free."

"I gotta run. A customer is about to walk in."

An older woman paused in front of Beth's store as I turned from the window. "Bye."

Herman perched on the back of the sofa. "I had much better taste in friends than Amos Branson."

Giving him a side eye, I picked up a dust cloth and a spray can of wax. "I'm not judging you for being chatty with the local cops. Sometimes, being nice to certain people is the right thing to do, but it doesn't indicate you're actually friends."

"True." He faded away. I wondered where he went when his ghostly form wasn't hovering around me. Not that it mattered unless other ghosts were lingering that I couldn't see. That was a question for another time.

I spent the next hour deep cleaning the front salon, dusting furniture, and vacuuming the cushions and drapes. Shoving the last sofa into place, I groaned and took in the spacious area. "One room is ready for customers." Herman's racks of dresses, still waiting for a buyer's love, drew me in. Color, fabric, and size organized each section, from casual to dressy—and then there were the gowns. Bridal, attendants, and mothers' dresses were in another section. I selected an ivory silk off the shoulder gown with a cinched jeweled waist. *You could gather the short chapel-length train for ease of walking or dancing.* I pressed it against my body and gazed into the mirror.

The door opened and I turned.

Eddie strolled in, dressed in his police uniform.

"The dress suits you. Did you design it?"

I looked down, felt heat flush my cheeks, and hastily re-hung it. "Thank you, but no, it was Herman." I gestured to the racks. "These were his. I was thinking how best to feature them." Unexpected tears pricked my eyes. "He was very talented."

"You might want to keep that dress for someday." His eyes twinkled and a smile tugged at the corners of his mouth.

Brushing a stray lock of hair from my face, I smiled, "How can I help you?"

"I stopped by Beth's, and she mentioned you had a visitor earlier." There was an edge to his voice that hadn't been there moments before.

"My day has been filled with unexpected visits by the local police department." I tried to make light of the encounter.

"He told you to bypass the emergency number and call him directly if something concerned you?"

"Not that I would. If I were to call anyone, it would be Ethan and Beth. Or maybe you." I tipped my head to the side. "He said something that was puzzling."

"Oh?" The question lingered in the air.

"He insinuated I might not be held responsible for Mr. Prescott's untimely death. The evidence could point in a different direction, and I should call him Amos. But yesterday and this morning, he was determined to pin the murder on me. Are there new leads that would change his mind?"

"Not that I'm aware of. However, we could meet for dinner and discuss what I've discovered regarding the open questions you and Beth mentioned last night."

"Dinner?"

He laughed as I stuttered the word. "With Beth and Ethan, of course."

I nodded. "Sure. I can whip up something." This way, Herman could hear, too.

"Great. I'm off at four, and Beth closes at five. I've already checked with her and Ethan. They said they'll come over around six if it's okay with you?"

I glanced at my watch and noted I'd have time to do more cleaning and, after a quick shower, fix a meal. My dream of a long, hot shower evaporated like steam. I wasn't a great cook. "Does everyone like mac and cheese?" I didn't add that it was the only casserole my grandmother ate and enjoyed.

"Anything that doesn't come out of a box is fine dining to me." He winked. "I'll look forward to it. I'll bring dessert."

"You just said you don't cook."

"But Brewed Bliss has some great desserts that I can pick up after my shift."

With a grin, I said, "I'm partial to everything lemon."

He tapped his temple. "Got it. See you later."

I frowned as he closed the door. Every shop door needed a bell to announce visitors. "Herman, are you here?"

The drapes fluttered. "At your service."

"Why don't you have a bell on your door?" I pointed to the upper casing.

"I do." He tipped his head. "I did. How long has that been gone? You can see the holes in the wood where it used to be."

As I drew closer, I did. "You're saying you didn't take it down?"

"No. I wouldn't. If I were in the back, I'd know someone walked in." He cupped his chin in his hand. He floated from the room.

I continued to study the empty holes. "Herman?" I went into the workroom, where he was reclining on the worktable. "Is it possible that whoever pushed you down the stairs removed the bell so you wouldn't hear them enter the shop?"

"Before you go down that path, ask Ethan what he knows about it being missing. Maybe it was annoying me, so I took it down."

I pulled out the desk chair and sat. "How likely do you think that is?"

"I've had that bell since the day after I opened."

I twirled in the chair, opening and closing desk drawers and file cabinets to search for it. "If you removed the bell, don't you think it would be here?"

He hovered near my arm. "I wouldn't throw out something that was in perfectly good condition. If anything, I would have given it away."

A packet of photos was in the center drawer of the desk. "What are these?"

"For certain dresses that I wanted to showcase in an advertisement, I'd take pictures of the bride modeling them. Take a gander—there are some humdingers."

I smiled at the old-fashioned phrase. Herman was cute as a button, even if he was a ghost. We would have gotten along if I'd had the chance to work with him. Flipping through the images, stunned at the intricacy of the gowns. Tapping one picture, I said, "This lace is exquisite." I peered closer. "Herman, look, there's the bell above the door."

"Told you there was a bell."

"When was this picture taken?" Turning it over, I said, "It's dated November of last year."

"That was right before my accident." He moved away as if it were hard for him to look at the photos. "I never had the chance to use it to promote the shop."

"The dress is beautiful. At least you delivered it before, well, you know." I hated to keep talking about the accident or his death. It had to be hard enough being a ghost in a holding pattern while he waited for the police to solve his murder.

"Barbie was a beautiful bride."

I turned the desk lamp on and studied the bride's face. "Barbara Hall?"

"She's a bit cheeky, and her friends who stood up with her are just as bad. They've been like that since they came here for their prom dresses; money was never an issue. They liked what they liked and bought it."

I set the picture down. "Are you talking about Kasey Pelham and Julie Clinton?"

"Those are the girls. Do you know them?"

"We formally met yesterday at the grocery store."

"They like to spend money, so be polite when you see them. They always gave me glowing recommendations to everyone who was looking to buy a nice dress. You can't afford to lose their business."

"They were also at Mr. Prescott's house right after the police arrived, trying to finagle their way inside. More like they were trying to get the dirt on what had happened." I thought about the claim of the woman seen entering Prescott's house the night before. Could one of them have been the unidentified witness? It was something to bring up over dinner.

"Claudia, could you start organizing in here?"

"I want to finish the dressing rooms. I was almost done when I got distracted by Amos, then Eddie and the confirmation of the missing bell. I have plenty of time. It's not like I'm opening on Monday, but taking the slow and methodical approach allows me to become acquainted with the feel of the space I'll be creating in, getting the vibe."

"An excellent idea. I'd been here so long I never thought you'd need to make it your own."

"It's like a new apartment, not like me moving in upstairs, but when all the walls are bare, and there's no furniture, it takes time to discover a space's personality."

"I get it. I want you to be happy and successful. Don't make the shop or the apartment a shrine to this old man."

I wished I could hug Herman, but I had to settle for conversation. "I love how you've furnished the apartment. When I get time, I'll donate your clothes and replace the curtains throughout except for my room. It's perfect."

The front door slammed. I jumped up. "I really should have locked that door. Now, who's here?"

15

came out of the back room. The troublesome trio stood in the middle of the shop. I kept a smile to myself as I said, "Hello, ladies. I'm not open for business yet."

Barbara said, "That's okay. We know you're not open to regular customers, but we're special. Herman made my wedding dress; it was stunning. Are you as talented as he was? He knew how to make a dress that fit my curves perfectly." She ran her hand over her waist and hips.

Unsure how to answer the question of talent, I wished Herman would pop in and feed me a couple of lines.

She cocked a brow. "Hello?"

"I'm sorry, Barbara." She smiled when I used her name. "As you can imagine, my life has been a little chaotic since I arrived in town. I'm just now starting to get the shop ready."

"That's fine." She had a nasal whine in her voice. "What about your ability to create stunning dresses? We like to make an entrance wherever we go."

Kasey and Julie's heads bobbed in unison.

"My uncle had years of experience, but I hope you'll allow me to show you what I can design. What I lack in years of experience I make up for in being fashion forward."

They glanced at my jeans and shirt and frowned. "Present outfit excluded?"

"Before coming to Drakes Bay, I worked in a top fashion house in New York City. Jeans are great for cleaning." I shouldn't have to explain myself, so I kept my tone pleasant. "When was the last time you were in the shop?"

"Me?" Barbara asked.

"All of you. I was wondering if there was a bell on the door. There are holes in the casing, so I guessed there must have been one at some point."

Kasey scrunched her face as if I'd asked a difficult question. "Yes, now that you mention it, there was a cute little brass bell that hung from a leather strap."

Julie nodded. "It was an old-fashioned touch. Whimsical."

"What happened to it? Did you take it down?" Barbara asked.

"I'm not sure." I frowned. "I didn't take it down and I'll reinstall it if I can find it."

Julie snapped her fingers. "If you can't, try Twice Loved. It's a cute second-hand shop down the street. Fiona Doyle owns it and has the best inventory. I'll bet she's got the perfect bell—that is, if you don't find the original."

"I appreciate the tip. Does she have vintage clothing?"

Kasey wrinkled her nose. "Like used dresses?"

"That's right. Beautiful buttons, lace, or a garment can be transformed into something lovely." I was passionate about upcycling previously loved clothes, and it would be a part of my business.

"If you say so." Barbara sniffed as she looked around the room. "Can I ask an indelicate question?"

She already had. I was curious what they had on their mind since it was apparent they weren't here to shop. "What can I help with?"

"Where was Herman found? I mean, was it messy?"

Taken aback by the questions regarding Herman's death, I

stammered. "I don't know. That happened months ago, and I didn't ask Ethan or Beth. Why do you want to know?"

"It was the first time someone died under mysterious circumstances that we knew, well, until Colton's murder." A gleam came in Kasey's eyes. "You saw him. How did he look? Was it like on television? Did you want to toss your cookies?"

I pressed my hand to my midsection. "I'm not supposed to talk about what I saw since it's an active investigation. Officer Branson wouldn't like it."

Barbara smirked. "Don't worry about Amos. His bark is worse than his bite. Besides, we go *way* back, and he wouldn't mind if you shared the details with us."

They laughed and looked at each other.

"Am I missing something?"

Julie said, "Amos has had a thing for Barbara since grade school. He used to follow her around like a puppy. Heck, he even thought she'd marry him someday. That was until Knox swept her off her feet."

"It didn't hurt he was loaded." Kasey laughed.

"Just as easy to marry for money as love." Barbara sighed. "I got lucky and found both in the same guy."

"How did Amos take the news?"

"He was understandably upset. I broke it to him gently when I gave him back his promise charm."

"What's that?" I was genuinely interested. I had heard of a promise ring but never a charm.

"You've seen them at different fairs, I'm sure." Barbara said, "It's a charm with two halves that make a whole. You each carry a half or wear it as a charm on a necklace—just a cheap piece of costume jewelry. We'd dated but weren't exclusive. I shouldn't have accepted it. Amos got the wrong idea and was upset when Knox and I started dating." She gave me the once-over. "You might want to consider going out with him. He pulls a lot of overtime, and I happen to know for a fact he's built up his bank account."

I wasn't sure how any of this was relevant to my current situation. "I don't have time to date."

She lifted a shoulder and shrugged. "You could do worse."

While the ladies were looking to exchange tidbits, getting useful information from them might be possible. "Did you ladies know Mr. Prescott well?"

"Not really. We all live on the same street, but he wasn't very friendly and kept to himself. Right after he moved in, he planted those shrubs so no one could see his house."

"Did you see anyone out of the ordinary in your neighborhood two nights ago?"

"I didn't." Julie pressed her hand to her chest. "I took the dogs out around eleven, and the street was deserted."

"When I pulled the shades in the living room, I saw the police cruiser drive past. They're like clockwork in our area. Four times a day. It's part of the agreement with the police and our neighborhood watch group." Kasey said.

My heart rate ticked up. "What time was that?"

She said, "They come at two-thirty and ten-thirty a.m. and p.m."

"Did any of you see lights on at Mr. Prescott's?"

Julie frowned. "They weren't on when I went outside which is weird. He never turns them off until midnight."

Barbara remained mum while Kasey and Julie shared. "Barbara, did you notice anything?"

"I went to bed early. I had a headache."

"And your husband?"

"Knox is out of town on business. Are you accusing me of something, Claudia?" Annoyance flickered in her eyes.

"Oh, my heavens, no. I was wondering if he saw or heard anything, that's all. The more information that can be provided to the police, the better chance of solving this crime quickly."

Her eyes and lips softened. "This entire matter has been

very upsetting. I didn't mean to snap. Knox will be home on Friday, so I'll feel better. We can be vigilant, but if someone could enter Mr. Prescott's home and shoot him in cold blood in his study, well, they could do it to any of us."

"Did you hear the gunshot?" This time, I kept my tone more gossipy and less inquisitive.

"We've talked about that," Julie said. "We can't place the sound of a vehicle backfiring, which is what Amos told Barbara it would have sounded like, at any point in between the end of the day and when you were found hovering over the body the next morning." The unasked question lingered in the air.

I wanted to correct their picture of the crime scene, but it was privileged information. I would keep my lips zipped until I saw a detailed account of what happened in the news-paper. I held my hands up. "I'm sorry. I wish I could tell you what I saw, but I'm not taking any chances with the law. However, I will tell you it was a shock to my system. I'm still reeling from everything."

"You haven't said when you're going to reopen?" Kasey jabbed Julie in the ribs and bobbed her head to Barbara's pale and drawn face.

"The first of next month."

Julie slipped her arm through Barbara's. "Are you all right?"

She nodded. "I just got a flash of what Claudia must have witnessed." Her eyes met mine. "That was horrible. I'm sorry it happened to you."

Why was she apologizing to me? At least she wasn't accusing me of killing Prescott. Could she have seen some-thing and figured out what it was and how it would connect to the crime?

"I'll be fine, but thank you."

She turned to her friends. "We should go." Forcing a smile, she said, "Don't forget to wander by Twice Loved and tell Fiona we sent you." They walked to the door and didn't look back as Kasey closed it after them.

What had Barbara remembered? It wasn't picturing a dead body that freaked her out. I crossed the room and flipped the deadbolt. There was no way anyone else would wander in today.

Something was niggling at me about when I found Prescott. Other than the house being cold, which I concluded was to keep the body from decaying quickly, that could mean he died earlier in the day and not later that night. Another question for Ethan and Eddie. How could I convince Eddie to share specific details about the crime scene? Would he give me access to any pictures taken?

Julie said there were no lights on at Prescott's around eleven. He had to have been already dead.

As I climbed the stairs to my apartment, I contemplated how best to ask Eddie these essential questions. Once upstairs, I put the instant tea kettle on and texted Beth.

Could you come over early? I have a few ideas to bounce off you…

Minutes later, she responded. *I can be there by five.*

I sent the sleuth emoji, waited four minutes until the water was hot, added a drizzle of honey to my mug of tea, and strolled into the living room. It was comforting to discover the apartment already felt like home. Lola stretched across a sofa cushion and rolled to her back. I paused to rub her tummy while perusing the clues we had uncovered.

Thinking back, I had knocked over a chair and some folders when I rushed out of the study. Prescott had a chain in his hand. Too bad I didn't know what it was. Could it have been a rosary? Otherwise, everything seemed like a typical home office. Did the police find the contract Herman had supposedly been amenable to?

I set the mug down, picked up a marker, and added those

questions under the Prescott column. Crossing my arms over my body, I stared at the board and added, *missing bell* under Herman. It might be a stretch, but in the movies, the killer would have taken the bell down before attacking so the victim couldn't hear them coming, especially if it were premeditated.

"I still don't get why would someone want to kill Herman?"

"Are you talking to me or you?" My friendly ghost drifted to the window seat. "I've been thinking, why would someone want me dead? Don't ask me why, but when Amos was here earlier and implied we were friendly, I got to thinking."

He had my full attention.

"Bear with me, my memory is a bit fuzzy."

"Maybe it's the new version of you."

"You become a ghost and see how clear your thoughts are." He looked out the window.

Instantly, I regretted poking fun at him. "I'm sorry, Herman, continue."

"Anyway, when Barbara said Amos was a good catch because he had money, it jiggled something in my noggin."

I wanted to beg him to get to the point, but rushing anyone, no matter how young, old, ghostly, or living, was rude. "Don't worry. I don't intend to date Amos."

"Good." He gave a brisk nod. "As I was saying, if he's got a nice bank account, how did he get it? Working overtime in a small town wouldn't significantly feather a nest. I'm taking a leap; he was getting juice money."

"He's selling juice as a side business?"

"No. What did they teach you in school? Juice is slang for extortion."

"That's preposterous. A small-town cop is walking around asking small businesses to pay him for what?"

"To keep the peace, a watchful eye, that kind of thing."

"Did you?" My blood hummed in my veins. If Amos

Branson had taken money from businesspeople to provide enhanced protection, he would not have gotten one red cent from me.

"I don't think I would. Check the financial records. If I had there would be a notation somewhere."

"Would he have killed you if you didn't pay up?"

"That I can't answer. Before your friends get here, look through my ledger book. If it's anywhere, it would be there."

"I haven't found it. Did you keep your finances on the computer?"

He looked as if he tried to snap his fingers and frowned. "Yes, I converted a few years ago to help my accountant."

"You said being a ghost dulled your memory. But you're pretty sharp."

"I might not remember who killed me. However, the details of my business, which is now your business, are important. Since you arrived, I've been racking my brain to remember all I can to help you."

"That's sweet. I wish you could remember the most important detail; who harmed you? It could be the key to discovering Prescott's killer, too."

"You're convinced the two are related?" Herman drifted to the sofa, and Lola curled up in a ball close to what would have been his legs.

"I am. Tomorrow, I'm going to the second-hand shop to find a new bell for the door. After today, I'm convinced someone took it down without your knowledge so that when they entered the shop, you wouldn't notice."

"Wouldn't they have come in through the upstairs door? I fell from top to bottom, which means I was pushed from my kitchen."

"True, but a customer would come in the front. If a passerby on the sidewalk saw them, it wouldn't be out of the norm, right? But if someone who shouldn't be here came up the back stairs, that would raise suspicion."

"I understand your line of reasoning. You should discuss this with Ethan over dinner, including the part about the bell. He might have information on what happened to it."

I sank to a chair and leaned forward, my hands between my knees and my shoulders slumped. "Herman, are you sure Ethan is trustworthy? If Amos is making business owners pay him money for so-called protection, which seems unlikely since Drakes Bay isn't a hot spot of crime, as the former chief, he might have been in on the scheme."

"Not a chance. I'd stake my mortal soul on his reputation. You can trust Ethan. He's as honest as they come."

Eddie may be the weak link. I left Herman snuggling with Lola and went to take a shower. Maybe the steam would help extract my jumbled thoughts.

16

$\mathcal{A}$t five on the dot, I heard footsteps running up the back steps and a rap on the door. I glanced at the camera app and saw it was Beth. "Come in," I yelled from the kitchen. I had unlocked the door moments before.

"Just me." I heard the door close firmly and then the stomping of her boots. She popped around the corner in stocking feet carrying a tissue-wrapped package.

"You didn't need to bring anything for dinner." I finished shredding the cheese and wiped my hands on a towel.

"It's not dinner." She handed it to me. "A little something to welcome you to town."

"You didn't have to get me anything." I took the package, which squished under my fingertips.

"Open it," she beamed.

I folded the tissue back. Inside was a deep purple knitted beret and a matching scarf. "These are beautiful," I said, touching the petal-soft wool.

"I haven't finished the mittens yet, but they should be ready in a day or so, depending on how busy the store is."

"You made these?"

"Of course. I didn't run to the store and buy them." She shuddered playfully and laughed. "What kind of knitting shop owner would I be?" Taking the scarf, she draped it around my neck and placed the hat on my head. "Go look in the mirror. The color's perfect, and it'll go with your winter coat."

This morning, I noticed a long mirror inside the front hall closet. I peered at my reflection. "This is the prettiest hat and scarf I've ever owned."

She grinned, pleased with my sincere compliment.

I took them off and placed them in a basket inside the closet I had claimed for hats and gloves. This set was special, and I'd wear them often. I shut the door. "Wine?"

"Love some. I'm dying to know why you asked me to come over before the guys. Did you learn something else other than Amos being a butthead?"

I gestured to the board. "Have a look, and I'll get the wine and join you once I slide the casserole into the oven."

She wandered to the front windows and sat in the window seat while she stroked Lola's head. "Did I see you grating cheese?"

"You did. I don't cook many things well. This mac and cheese recipe has been perfected, and I put in the extra effort regarding the cheese."

"Mine come from a little yellow box. It's easy. I boil the noodles, add milk, butter, and the powdered cheese packet. Stir, wait for it to congeal, and enjoy."

"That works, too, when I'm cooking for myself—but for friends, I have to go authentic." I carried two glasses of red wine and passed one to Beth. "I wasn't sure what vintage to use with comfort food, so I'm serving what I like to drink."

She tapped my glass with hers. "Cheers." Nodding to the board, she sipped her wine. "You've been busy."

"The trio stopped in to see me when I was cleaning the shop. I think they have credit cards getting dusty and are itching to use them. I found some notes from Herman, and it seems they were frequent shoppers."

"That doesn't surprise me. Herman made Barbara's wedding dress."

"So I heard." I sipped my wine. "Do you remember a bell hanging above the front door?"

"Yes. I added one when I realized how useful it was if you were in another room. Why?"

"I see holes where it was, but the bell is MIA."

Her forehead crinkled. "Really? You should ask Dad about it. He might know. He was always puttering around the store. He liked to help Herman. Tell me what else the ladies had to say."

"Well," I sat down. "Barbara and Amos were a couple until she met Knox, who, she made sure I knew, had a healthy bank account, unlike a cop's salary."

"Snob. Cops make a decent living. Just because Amos couldn't drench her in diamonds and designer clothes didn't mean he wouldn't be a good partner."

"Is that why he's sour on life?"

"Most likely. He followed her around for years and she let him. It was painful to watch the fallout when she dumped him. I felt sorry for the guy. Do you think that has anything to do with the case?"

"No, just an observation. The most interesting details were about the night Prescott was killed. I'm certain now he was killed in the early evening."

She crossed the room and sat next to me. "Tell me everything."

"The ladies talked about their neighborhood watch program and the police driving through there four times per day, at the same times, two-thirty and ten-thirty."

"There's an established pattern." She tapped the glass with her fingernail. "If the killer were paying attention, he'd know when the coast was clear."

"Exactly. The neighbors knew Mr. Prescott's lights went dark at midnight, but they were already off when Julie took her dogs out at eleven. If the killer didn't know that part of the routine, he would have doused the lights to cover his tracks. If the lights were left on all night, it would be a red flag."

"Potentially, someone would call the police for a wellness check." She said, "Eddie will have an interesting insight into this theory because if I'm following you, Prescott was killed earlier. I presume after dark and around the time you received the call."

"That's what I think. Whoever killed Prescott called me to make sure I'd go to the house and find the body, and whoever it was called in the gunshot to the police to set me up to take the heat off them during the investigation. There's still the question of the phone call to Amos about a gunshot in the morning. The ladies said they didn't hear anything so it couldn't have been one of them."

With a snap of her fingers, she frowned. "That must be a hoax." She crossed to the kitchen.

I shook my head. "It was the killer executing their carefully planned frame-up. What about that truck we saw roar past us when we were sitting in front of the house? Is it possible that's connected to all of this?"

"No." She returned with the wine bottle, adding a splash to our glasses. "It was just a truck passing. Prescott was already dead, so the culprit wasn't rushing from the scene."

"What if that person waited for me to arrive and called in the supposed gunshot."

"That's probable."

Each lost in our own thoughts, and I let my mind wander. I needed to talk this out from the beginning. "Before the guys arrive, can we walk through everything that's happened from the start and see what makes sense and what doesn't?"

"You have the floor." With laser focus, she studied my face. "You know how this could have happened, don't you?"

"I think so. It started to come together when Amos was here earlier, something he said got me thinking."

Shifting on the sofa, she leaned back. Lola jumped into her lap and purred. I walked a few steps and turned around, trying to figure out where to begin.

"It started when Herman was contacted about selling the shop. We haven't found evidence of a contract, so that's a question for Eddie. Was anything found here or at the Prescott house that would support Herman and Prescott were in negotiations? Herman was pushed to his death and today I find this in the stairway." I pulled the half of a shamrock from my pocket. "My family isn't Irish so I'm taking a leap, but this didn't belong to Herman. No one else would have been on the inside stairs, so it's logical the killer dropped it."

I handed it to Beth, who turned it over in her hand. "This isn't an expensive piece of jewelry."

"Now, let's talk about the bell. The killer could have, at some point, removed it, planning on sneaking in the front door to confront Herman. My guess is that Colton Prescott wanted to get his hands on this property one way or the other. They argue. Prescott pushes Herman, who falls to his death. In his haste to leave, he drops the charm. For the record, Colton Prescott is an Irish name, so that clue fits."

"Colton Prescott kills your uncle. Who killed Prescott and why?"

I sucked in my lower lip, about to cast a shadow on the local police department, the one Ethan had supervised for a long time. I didn't feel I had a choice. "After Amos left, I dug into my uncle's files. I didn't find anything to corroborate this, but let the idea percolate." I paused. "Amos implied that I should call him directly if I needed backup. He also mentioned I might not be guilty of killing Prescott and that we would chat regularly and, like Herman, I'd never have any trouble."

"A strong police presence does keep the bad guys guessing."

"I felt like I was being primed to ask for a personal donation." I had gone this far, so I said, "If he wanted a contribution for the police department, he wouldn't give me a private cell phone number. It's doesn't make sense."

Her mouth gaped open. "Are you saying you think we have a dirty police department?" She jumped to her feet and glared at me.

"Beth," I stepped toward her. "I'm not saying the department is, but Amos might be. Barbara said he had a healthy bank account, as if that was some criteria for dating him. She said he got it from a lot of overtime. Is that possible?"

A knock on the door drew our attention.

"Do you plan on asking my father about this?"

I exhaled. "I have to. I think it's relevant to both cases; I'm just not sure how yet."

She crossed her arms over her chest. "He's going to be insulted, and Eddie will be furious."

"If we can't talk openly about ideas, why are we even trying to solve Herman's death?"

Another knock on the door. I hurried to the entrance and waved Ethan and Eddie inside. "Come in." I took their coats. "Beth's in the living room."

Eddie said, "Something smells good." He held up a box. "I hope you like pie."

I smiled. "As long as I didn't have to bake, it's my favorite kind." I took it. "Wine, beer, or something else?"

"Whatever you're having. I'll will take wine, if you have a bottle open." He smiled and went inside.

I detoured to the kitchen, checked the oven, and got glasses for him and Ethan. When I crossed into the living room, the conversation died. Beth wouldn't look at me, and Eddie's eyes fixed on me.

"You've heard about my suspicion?" I handed them each a glass and then poured the ruby red liquid.

Ethan cleared his throat and scowled. "It's concerning to hear that you might believe any police officer is attempting to extort money from shop owners."

There was no way I could say I found something in writing from Herman when I hadn't. "Don't you think it was odd what he said? Telling me not to call 9-1-1 for help but to contact him directly?"

Eddie glanced at Ethan and then at me. "You need to let this go."

"Why?"

He groaned. "You have no reason to trust me, but please, take a leap of faith."

Beth's eyes were wide as she nodded. "We should focus on the shamrock you found. There are questions you wanted to ask Eddie about Prescott's house."

Herman drifted in. "You can trust these people with your life."

How could I know for sure? I was tired of him taking their side constantly. It would have been easier to talk to his ghost via telepathy, but that wasn't an option. "Should I encourage Amos?"

Eddie shook his head. "No." The word came out like a whip and enhanced the tension in the room. "Stay away from him."

My insides clenched. "I was right to be concerned."

Ethan touched my shoulder. "Claudia, there are times when it's best not to know what is happening. But I'm glad you spoke up."

"You're not angry with me?" I glanced at Beth, knowing how upset she had been.

"Not at all. I considered your uncle one of my best friends.

If he were here, he'd tell you that I'm an honest person, trust-worthy and loyal. But I'm not stupid. If someone breaks the law, in time, the law will catch up to them."

I picked up my glass. "All right. I can do that." The liquid inside sloshed from side to side as I wished I could calm my nerves.

Eddie put a steady hand on mine. "Tell me about Prescott and Herman. On the board, you've written something about a missing bell?"

I cleared my throat. "Right. The bell. I found some pictures in the desk of ladies in bridal gowns. Herman must have taken them at the final fittings. In all of them, he used the front of the shop as the backdrop, and there was a bell above the door. I've seen the holes, but it's missing. It might not be important, but what happened to it?"

Ethan said, "I might have a partial answer. On that night in November, the lights were on in the dress shop. It was well after closing time, and it was unlike Herman to keep the shop open late. I stopped over to check on him and discovered the front door was unlocked. I entered and tripped on a leather strap near the door. That's when I found Herman. I never thought about it again until now, but that must have suspended the bell from the hanger."

"How long do you think he lay there?"

"Are you sure you want to hear this? It'll be hard on you."

I blinked away the tears that filled my eyes. "It's impor-tant to know what happened. Did he suffer?"

"It had been a couple of hours. He looked peaceful."

At least that was comforting. I wouldn't want to think of Herman in pain and alone lying on the floor helpless. "The bell wasn't found?"

He shook his head. "Not that I know of."

I had said the phrase, what if, way too many times tonight, but I was about to do it again. "What if whoever pushed Herman cut the bell down so it wouldn't alert him as they entered the shop? There was an argument, and when he was pushed, their lucky charm fell on the stairs."

Beth handed her father the half charm.

"Prescott was Irish. I think he killed my uncle for this shop, dropped the charm, and his killer found out and attempted to blackmail him."

Ethan said. "They might have argued that night. Things got out of hand."

"Flash forward, whoever might have been trying to blackmail Prescott argued with him and during the fight, he mentioned a meeting with you to convince you to sell the dress shop." Eddie said, "Pinning the crime on you was convenient."

"Which leads me to questions only you can answer, Eddie, and since you've asked me to trust you, I'm asking you to do the same and help wrap up a few details."

He shook his head. "This is a bad idea."

"You and Ethan agreed to the sofa sleuths helping." I cocked my head. "What do you say?"

17

———

"Can we eat first?" Eddie asked. "My brain works better with fuel."

A nervous giggle escaped Beth's lips. "Claudia, I'm sorry for getting defensive before."

"It's okay. I would have reacted the same way if someone was poking at my family's vocation."

Diplomatically, Ethan asked, "What's for dinner?"

I liked how he attempted to steer the conversation in a new direction. "Macaroni and cheese, salad, and pie." I gestured to the table. "Take a seat." I placed the salad bowl and dressing on the table and removed the casserole dish from the oven. When I looked up, Eddie had put the dry-erase board in the corner of the room.

He gave me a wink. "Dinner conversation."

"Beth said you made a good dent in the shop today?" Ethan added a dash of pepper to his salad.

"In between visitors, the front and dressing rooms are set. Tomorrow, I'll tackle the workroom and continue to organize the desk. Herman was a whiz with a needle and thread, but paperwork? Not so much."

"Hey, I resent that." Herman sat on the counter.

"It seems he had a logical system, so it'll be easy to understand once I dig in. We look at business from different perspectives. I had an entire semester in design school about keeping an office humming."

"When I opened this shop, I didn't need to be a paper-pushing whiz kid. But I understand what you're saying. I hated paperwork unless it was tissue paper." He gave a ghostly chuckle.

Now, my ghost was showing his sense of humor.

"That's great. You're still planning on opening in a few weeks?" Eddie rolled his eyes back. "This macaroni is so creamy."

I smiled at Beth, and she returned it with a grin. "Thank you."

We spent several more minutes enjoying dinner as my eyes drifted back to the board. I wanted to dive into my questions about evidence. Based on Eddie's enjoyment of dinner, if I had food, I had a captive audience who, at some point, might fill in the details.

After his second helping, he scraped the last of the cheese sauce from his plate and put his fork down. "The only thing that would make this better would be the addition of fresh lobster."

Ethan said, "The next time I get a deal, I'll buy some for you."

"And invite everyone for dinner again?" I chuckled. "Better yet, just make it a standing invite if someone gives me a couple of hours' notice and doesn't mind eating the same thing every time. This is my best dish."

Everyone chuckled as Beth cleared the dishes and stacked them in the sink. "Conversation, then dessert."

I took that as my opening since Ethan and Eddie didn't disagree. "Eddie, did you get a chance to check on the call log from yesterday?"

"I checked, but nothing came into the main line. I asked

Amos, who said the person called his cell phone, and the number was unavailable."

I cocked a brow. "Interesting." That needed to go on the board. Withdrawing a marker from my pocket, I pulled the board close and made a note under the Prescott column. "Did you and Amos arrive at the same time?"

"No. He was already inside when I pulled up. That part of town is his regular patrol area. I heard the call for assistance over the radio."

I nodded and made another note, prepared to come back to that later when I revealed what the trio said. "Did you find the contract Mr. Prescott mentioned to me?"

He shifted in his seat. "I feel like I'm on the witness stand. But no, there wasn't a contract on his desk nor in the papers we found on the floor, which I think you mentioned knocking over when you were rushing out to call for Beth."

"That's right. I bumped the table, and the papers went flying. I didn't stop to pick them up."

"She was understandably freaked out." I heard Beth's protective tone and was grateful for her support, even though we were among her family and my new friends.

Eddie nodded. "Continue, Counselor."

"What was the necklace he had clutched in his hand?"

His eyes flickered with surprise, and he tipped his head to the side. "You're very observant."

"It helps in design to be mindful of details. Now, what was it?"

He glanced at Ethan, who inclined his head as if to agree that he could tell me. "On the board, you have noted a half charm. Is that what Beth showed us earlier?"

"It is."

Beth pushed away from the table. "I'll be right back."

Upon her return, she handed Eddie the piece. His eyes widened for a fraction of a moment, and he turned it over and gave it to Ethan. "Did you find a chain?"

"No. When I changed the lightbulb this morning, I saw it from the top of the ladder laying on the stairs... You recognize it, don't you?"

"It's similar, but I won't be certain until I have the pieces together; they might be two halves that make a whole."

"It was the charm." I leaned back. "Well, isn't that just a duck on a lake?"

He blinked hard. "What?"

"Sorry, something my grandmother said. This is the second time a charm has come up today."

Eddie leaned on the table. "Who else mentioned one?"

"Barbara Hall. She casually mentioned years ago that Amos bought her a promise charm with two halves."

"That was long before she met Knox Hall. Did she happen to say what kind of charm it was?"

Now, it was my turn to be surprised. I never connected Barbara's charm to this one. From her description it matched. I felt the color drain from my face. "Do you think Barbara Hall killed Herman and Prescott? She said she went to bed early because she had a headache, and her husband was on a business trip. Oh, my goodness." I pushed back from the table and fanned my face as I paced. "She doesn't have an alibi. And a woman could have called in the gunshot. She could have seen my Jeep from her house and waited for the perfect moment."

Beth guided me to the chair. "Sit down and put your head between your knees. Breathe in and out very slowly."

I did as she said. Ethan moved to the sink, ran the water, and placed a cool towel on my neck, keeping a soothing hand on my shoulder.

Eddie knelt before me. "Everything will be okay. Just try and relax."

I wanted to snap that he hadn't had a two-time murderer in his dress shop. "Why would she have wanted to kill

Herman? He made dresses for her, including her wedding gown." Hot tears burned my eyes.

"Claudia, look at me." He rubbed my icy hands in his.

I lifted my head and looked him in the eye. "Are you going to arrest her?"

He shook his head. "I don't have any evidence. Like you said, she has no motive to have wanted Herman dead. Even with her husband out of town and no one to vouch if she was home, I've got nothing concrete. She's living a comfortable life with her loving husband. Whoever ransacked Herman's office and bedroom was searching for something specific—not once but at least twice that we're aware of."

I sat up. "This goes back to Amos putting pressure on Herman for protection money, which means he's preying on people's fears."

Eddie shook his head. "Don't poke at that issue. That's not sofa sleuthing."

Beth said, "And those boot prints outside the back door were man-sized."

"If it gives you hollow comfort, Barbara didn't kill Herman. The evidence doesn't support the crime."

"What about the gun? Isn't that something a woman might use? Efficient and quick."

"I'm telling you things I shouldn't, but I want you to rest easy. Anyone can use a gun, and a .38 revolver is a common weapon. It's easy to handle even for a novice."

"Which is why I'm still a suspect despite Amos saying the case was moving in a different direction?"

A look passed between Eddie and Ethan. "Amos was trying to reassure you. Nothing more."

"Other than you finding the body, you were never considered a strong suspect. You had less motive than anyone in town. You never met Prescott. Ethan made that recording, which was brilliant, even if it couldn't be used in court. It gave you an ironclad alibi as far as the investigation went. In addition, Ethan had been around your shop during the day, and you never left the building. A former chief's statement carries a lot of weight."

I exhaled a sigh of relief. "That's good to know Amos was bluffing." I stood and stretched my arms over my head. "If Prescott killed Herman, what was he trying to find?"

Beth said, "The missing contract. If one existed, Herman would have torn it up. When Prescott searched the apartment after Herman fell, he didn't find it or took it with him."

My brain worked better when I had a distraction. "Dessert?" I dug through the drawers, found a knife, and sliced the lemon meringue pie. I glanced at Eddie through my lashes. He remembered.

I scooped out the first slice and paused. "Wait a second. If Prescott killed Herman and searched the building for the contract, then who came back while I was at Prescott's and searched the apartment again? You know, *Mr. I have boots with deep tread, guy*? That couldn't have been Prescott—he was already dead."

"I can't answer that," Eddie said. "There were no finger-prints other than yours and Beth's from cleaning, and the doorknob was wiped down."

"Someone knew I had the meeting with Prescott and came in after I left. It's the only thing that makes sense."

"What time did you leave?" Ethan asked.

"Before ten. Someone must have been waiting for me to go —unless I didn't notice the boot tracks coming from the alley, and they broke in before I came downstairs." I shuddered. "Could they have been watching me that entire time?"

"Did you hear anything before you left?"

"No."

"You never saw anyone?"

I shook my head. "I had started my Jeep a few minutes earlier, but all I noticed was the view of the bay."

"You left your Jeep running?" Ethan asked.

"Remote starter. I might be acting like a small-town girl, but I was raised in the suburbs, where people would steal a running vehicle. I'm very cautious."

Ethan nodded. "Good. How about we put aside the conversation about the two cases and enjoy this yummy-looking pie." He took the server from me and dished up three more slices.

My mind raced with the possibility Barbara wasn't who she appeared. She married for money and left the guy who loved her behind. Or had she? I spooned up the first bite and let the flavors dance over my taste buds.

Beth laughed. "Good, right? That's Nikki Twing for you. Perfection on a spoon or fork." Taking a bite herself, she said, "Eddie, good call on the pie."

"Thank you." He gave me a sly smile, and I kept quiet about the flavor choice. I could keep a secret when necessary.

"Beth, do you think Barbara loved Amos, and that's why he's morphed into this jerky man?"

Eddie said, "Why do you ask?"

"She married for money, not love. But she encouraged me to go out with him now that he's financially stable. Even though she said it, I didn't get the vibe she meant it."

Eddie cocked a brow. "The part about the money or that you should date him?"

"Oh, she meant it about the money. A gleam glinted in her eyes, but when I assured her I had more than enough to keep me busy with the new dress shop, she seemed almost relieved."

"Do you want to date Amos?"

Beth and Ethan stayed quiet while Eddie focused his attention on me.

"You're joking. He gives me the creeps. I couldn't wait for him to leave the shop. I even put the outside light on, hoping Beth would see it and call to check in."

"The outside light? Why?"

"Like a lighthouse beacon, guiding sailors safely into the harbor. It was the only thing that sprang to mind."

He grinned. "That was good thinking, but did she know it was a signal?"

I laughed. "Not at the time. It wasn't until after Amos left that she called. Now it's etched in stone. If that light goes on during the day, I need backup from Bess." I gave her a grin.

"Bess? Am I missing something?"

Beth laughed. "We're like Nancy Drew, Bess, and George if we were a threesome? Instead, I've adopted Bess as my alter ego, and Claudia is Nancy Drew."

He nodded, and Ethan said, "Oh no. You girls are the new version of those classic books?"

"Except we're not as young and we have jobs, a dress designer and handcrafter of knitwear. I think we are the perfect modern version."

I laughed. "You have to agree we do live in a small town. And, Ethan, you and Carson Drew are in the same line of work, sort of."

Eddie chuckled. "Who am I? Ned?"

I placed my hand on his arm, and my fingertips tingled. To my knowledge, Ned Nickerson wasn't a handsome police officer with blue-gray eyes that could turn from ice to a smolder in an instant. But I'd keep that little tidbit to myself. "Maybe you're an updated version, too."

Ethan said, "It suits me. I'll be on the sidelines helping to keep you out of trouble."

"Don't forget Beth and I are sofa sleuths. We can't get into any danger."

18

———

The following day, I woke refreshed. The sun was streaming in the windows; even though it was cold outside, it was toasty indoors. This was the first night I had slept solidly since arriving in Drakes Bay. As I lay in bed, Lola hovered in the doorway and meowed loudly, swishing her tail. I turned on my side and propped my hand under my head.

"Little girl, you sleep all day. Can't you give me one morning to lounge in bed?" I patted the sheets. "Come here."

Her tail darted from side to side, and she left. I laughed. "Guess she told me." It felt good to wake up happy. Today would be a great day. I flicked back the covers and shrieked as my feet hit the ice-cold floor. Hopping from one foot to the other, I hurried to the bathroom. First on my list was purchasing a rug for my room.

Once in the kitchen, I filled Lola's bowl with food, put on a pot of coffee, and made toast with peanut butter and banana. I had a legal pad on the table to create an organizational plan for the shop, but the board caught my eye. There was one thing I knew; I was keeping my distance from Barbara Hall.

"Herman, are you here?" I took my coffee and wandered into the living room. Perched in what I had decided was his usual spot on the window seat, he watched the street below.

Without looking at me, he said, "I miss going outside and strolling down the street to Brewed Bliss in the spring. I'd order a large mocha coffee and a bran muffin every day before I opened the shop. On Sundays, Sue Allen, who owns the place, would have a special of waffles, pancakes, French toast, or crepes, and in the warm months, there were tables out front so patrons could sit and watch the world go by. But you had to get there before the tourists to get a good spot."

I heard the nostalgia laced in his words. "You can't leave the building?"

He shook his head. "I've tried to slip through the doors, but it's like walking into a brick wall. Would you do me a favor?" He turned with his back to the window. "On Sunday, have breakfast at Brewed Bliss. Ask Beth to go with you and introduce you to Sue. It would mean a lot if you'd keep that tradition alive in my honor."

"Sure. I'll ask Beth today, and we'll make plans." My heart constricted for Herman. He had lost so much, and for what? Someone who was angry for an unknown reason? "Can we talk about the day you died?"

"We can, but we've gone over this several times and I'm not sure what else I can tell you."

"Do you know what time of day the accident happened?"

He drifted across the room and perched on the rocking chair. "You can ask Ethan what time he found me."

"He came over after the shop should have been closed, but that wouldn't be the same time as when you fell since he thought you'd been lying there for a couple of hours."

"Huh. Now that's interesting. I thought I died, and he found me right away. I guess time changes when you're watching yourself."

"What do you mean?" I sat down, coffee mug in my hands but not drinking.

"This is going to sound odd. As I left my body, I expected to see a comforting light that would draw me in. But I didn't. So, I sat next to my body and waited."

"Did you see anyone?" I leaned forward. This could be important.

"Not until Ethan arrived. He touched my wrist and then my neck. It was the first time I'd seen him cry except when his wife passed. He waited until Amos showed up, and the ambulance people took my body, but I stayed. I watched Amos pawing through my desk, and he put something in his pocket." Herman zipped around the room. "He took a card from my file drawer."

"What kind of card? A greeting card?"

"No. A white business card. Like the one he gave you."

"Why would he take it?"

Herman's face blossomed into a smile. "On the back, he had written how much I needed to give him monthly for my special protection, which I refused to pay. I remember something else." He seemed to pace; if alive, he'd be wearing a groove in the hardwood floor.

"What?"

"Ethan asked Amos why he came; he was off duty. That has to mean something."

"Was he dressed in his uniform?"

"I don't remember. However, he was in my apartment earlier. He swung by when he was on duty to chat."

I snapped my fingers. "That has to be it. He came by to put pressure on you to pay up. When you refused again, you argued."

"I told him I recorded our conversations. I was about to tear the card up in front of him. I headed down the stairs to get it." He shrugged, "I always did love the drama of grand gestures."

"Did he push you?" My heart was in my throat as I waited for confirmation of what I knew had to be true.

"No." Herman's ghostly form shrunk in size. "I tripped and fell. I heard his boots on the steps running down after me. He said I was going to be fine." My ghost stopped talking and sank on the window ledge again.

I waited for what felt like forever when I finally asked, "And Amos?"

"He left. When he returned, and my body was removed, he took the business card, but he wouldn't have had time to search for the tapes."

"Where did you stash them?"

"There aren't any. That's why he took the lead on the investigation and he's searched this building several times, and all he's gotten is frustration. At least in death, I found a way to repay him for how he treated me."

"Herman, this is great information, but there's no proof that he was here when you fell and never rendered aid. Where do I find the proof to prove he's culpable for your death?"

"Claudia, it's not up to you to solve the case. Ask Ethan more pointed questions that will trigger an idea. If Eddie's around, even better. They're very good at their job."

Now, I paced the same stretch of floor that Herman had. "If Amos allowed you to die, why kill Prescott?"

"That I can't answer. I still don't know why he wanted this storefront. Unless it was about the view."

"That doesn't fit." I chewed my fingernail.

"Sometimes people want what they can't have. Take a couple of hours this morning to chat up a few store owners. See if Prescott had approached any others with offers. That might lead you in a new direction for motive."

"I'm going to Twice Loved to see if there's a bell and maybe a vintage rug for my bedroom."

He smiled. "Fiona's a lovely, petite woman in her sixties,

maybe even seventy. She would never commit to an age. We had dinner once a month. I miss her blueberry pie."

A smile grew on my face. "Herman, were you a social butterfly around town?"

He shrugged. "I had my moments. Remember to ask her about Prescott. Weave it into the conversation, and tell her if there are other furnishings you're interested in. She can give you a first look as she gets new inventory."

"Thanks for the tip. Since I'm going out, I'd best bundle up."

The lights flickered on as I approached Twice Loved, a second-hand shop. The windows were full of treasures, both big and small. Confident I would find something for my place, I pulled open the glass-and-wood door. Soothing, soft piano jazz played in the background. No one greeted me, and I wondered where Fiona was.

I started on the outer perimeter. My fingers trailed over highly polished silver dishes, small wooden tables, and a velvet chair perfect for a dressing table that caught my eye. With the apartment well furnished, I didn't need much other than the bell for the shop and a rug, at least for now. Owning a store like this would have been a blast if I hadn't been a designer.

"Hello. Can I help you find something?" An older, petite, dark-haired woman walked toward me.

I stuck out my hand. "Hi, I'm Claudia Grant. I just moved to town and looking to add a few things to my place."

She clasped it between hers. "You're Herman's niece?"

"That's me." My smile faltered for a moment before regaining my composure. "Are you Fiona?"

"How did you know?" She laughed. "Because I'm the only person in the store?"

"Lucky guess." Herman had described her perfectly. Her smile was warm and genuine.

"Tell me what you're looking for, and then you can browse to your heart's content."

"I need a few things—a bell to put over a door and carpet for my bedroom. The floors are chilly. Also, do you carry vintage clothing?"

She smiled again. "I think I have the perfect area rug for your room. I helped Herman with several items when he had it redecorated for you. I might have a bell. Come with me."

I trailed behind her as she moved from the front to the middle of the shop and wandered down an aisle lined with shelves filled with knickknacks, the type of items someone might want to take home from a vacation or to furnish a beach house. She paused in front of a square metal table in the middle. It gave the shop a clear view, which is why she probably broke up the shelving units. Shoplifting could be a problem in a store like this.

"Here are a few bells," she said, handing me one. "This is a traditional shopkeeper's bell. It's affixed to the door, so whenever it opens, it jingles. Effective, but not a show-stopping piece." She then handed me a strand of tiny bells on a braided chain. "This hangs over the doorknob and looks pretty, but I think in your case, you wouldn't want anything snagging a garment on the way out the door. I'd avoid this one."

Glancing at her door, I said, "I noticed you don't have a bell."

"No, I have a silent alarm attached to my phone, which is always in my pocket. I'm not a fan of bells. But Herman loved the old-fashioned touch."

I didn't know that about him, but it made sense, given some of the antiques in the apartment. "I'll take the traditional bell."

She touched my hand. "Herman would have loved that. Now, let's go to the back room and check for that area rug.

You can peruse several racks of vintage clothing when we're done."

"Do you have a problem with theft?"

"It ebbs and flows, but I have a pretty good sense of whether someone who walks in the door likes a five-finger discount or wants to spend money."

"Does Amos pop in and check on things?"

She gave me a sharp look. "Why do you ask?"

I needed to appear casual when I wanted to pounce. "He stopped into the dress shop yesterday and gave me a card with his number. In case I ever needed help, I should call him."

"If you need something, call the department. Don't trust that guy. He's a man who comes with a lot of strings."

"Good to know."

She flipped over a few rugs stacked on top of each other. Finally, she said, "Here it is."

It had a cream background with a pale blue border, filled with roses in puddles of cream. She was right; this was perfect.

"Do you know what the dimensions are?"

"I happen to know it will fit your room. I picked it up with you in mind."

This would be my only chance to broach the Prescott topic, and I hoped it wouldn't sound abrupt. "What if I hadn't stayed?"

"I never thought that would happen. Even when Colton Prescott came around trying to buy my store and boasted he was sure you'd sell the minute you arrived. Herman was certain Grants Gowns would thrive under new management."

"Prescott wanted to buy your place, too?"

"Not just mine but the inn between us. Between you and me, I think he planned to raze the three properties and put up an ugly motel or take the inn and expand onto our land." She clucked her tongue and crossed her arms over her chest. "There was no way I was selling out, and Herman told him to go pound sand."

"What about the inn's owners? Were they interested?"

"Doubtful. Oliver and his wife, Mariah, just took it over from his parents. They're the third generation to run Whistler's Inn and Restaurant. Prescott needed all three properties to succeed, but hoped one might pressure the other two, if you catch my drift."

"I do." That tied up one mystery of why Prescott was so anxious to get his hands on the shop. "He didn't make a run for other buildings in town?"

"It was all about the bayside. Maybe eventually, but now it's a moot point since someone ended his negotiations permanently." She took the bell from my hand. "Do you want the rug? I can have my handyman deliver it next week."

"Yes, I would. Do you mind if I come back to look at the clothing? I still have two more places to stop before I roll up my sleeves and get the workroom spotless."

"Certainly. I'll ring up these two items. When I've talked to Beau Tinker, I'll give you a call when he can deliver. If you need any repairs done at your place, he's your guy."

"Thank you, Fiona. It's been so nice to meet you."

"Likewise. If you ever want to have a meal together, let me know. Herman and I tried to get together monthly. I've missed that."

"It sounds lovely, and we will get together soon." I paid for the bell and carpet, left the store, pulled my new scarf tight to my neck, and headed to Brewed Bliss. It was time for an introduction and coffee.

19

———

I came around the corner with my head down against the bracing wind and ran into a solid wall of man. "Oaf, I'm sorry." I pushed my hat back from my eyes. Amos and Barbara stood before me. "Hello."

He gave me a curt nod and grunted what could have been a hello, but I wasn't sure.

Barbara grumbled, "Watch where you're going, you big jerk." She shoved Amos aside and walked in the opposite direction.

I watched her storm off. "She's not having a good day."

Amos didn't respond but hurried after her. I waited another minute until he caught up to Barbara, grabbed her arm, and whirled her around. Then, I watched her crumple against his chest, and he wrapped his arms around her, walking them both to the doorway of the ice cream shop.

I'd have to ask Beth about what might have occurred. It was odd, considering they were formerly in a relationship, but that was long ago. Or was it?

The door to the coffee shop swung open. A young man stepped out and held the door for me. I walked into the surprisingly spacious area, which resembled a café. Scattered tables filled the front, with a counter in the back.

Several people were in line near the cash register. A tall, dark-haired woman greeted each person with a friendly smile, took their order and payment, and handed them a plastic number. It wasn't long before it was my turn.

"Hello." I scanned the menu. "I'll take two medium coffees with cream and sugar on the side. Wait, make that three, as well as two each of the sunshine and blueberry muffins, and they're to go." Ethan would probably be at the store, so getting something for him would be a small gesture of thanks for all he'd done for me.

"Are you Claudia Grant?"

I handed her my debit card. "Yes. Herman's niece."

"Welcome to town! I'm Sue Allen, and Brewed Bliss is my little slice of heaven. I was curious when you'd wander in from the cold."

"Things have been a little hectic since I arrived."

She gave me a solemn nod and handed me my card and a plastic number. "I heard. I'm sorry you've had to deal with that nonsense." Dropping her voice, she glanced around, saying, "Amos Branson let that badge swell his head. Don't pay any attention to him. If you're related to Herman, there's no way you'd hurt that nasty Colton Prescott."

"I appreciate your vote of confidence." I looked to see if I was the last customer for the moment, and I was. "He was ready to slap the cuffs on and charge me with murder."

She sniffed. "Of course he was, anything to make his job easier. The rest of the police force wouldn't let that happen, especially Chief Durgin. He's a sensible man, or you can always let Ethan know."

"Have you ever had any trouble with Amos? Yesterday, he stopped by the shop and told me we'd chat regularly."

Her eyebrows shot to her hairline. "He did what? Tell

Ethan Stewart. He'll put a stop to all that nonsense, and you don't listen to him. Better yet, keep your distance."

I wanted to continue the conversation, but the barista handed me a white bag and a coffee tray with my order. "Thanks, Sue. It was nice to meet you."

"Likewise. Stop by anytime. I serve a special plated breakfast every Sunday from seven to eleven. Otherwise, it's hand-held foods only."

As I threaded through the tables to the door, I could feel Sue's eyes on me. I turned, and she gave me a brisk nod. Unsure what to make of it, I crossed the street and made a beeline for Knit or Purl.

Ethan popped up from behind a counter when I closed the door. His face morphed into a warm smile. "Claudia, it's good to see you." He took the coffee tray. "You've met Sue?"

"I did. Also, Fiona Doyle from Twice Loved. I found a bell and an area rug for my apartment." I held up the paper bag before setting it on the counter.

"You've had a busy morning. Beth just ran upstairs, but she'll be right back."

I stuck my hat and scarf in my pockets and shrugged my jacket off as Ethan placed the muffins on paper napkins.

"This is a nice treat."

"After everything you and Beth have done for me since I arrived, it's the least I could do."

"You made dinner." He smiled, "And it was delicious."

"Thank you." I strolled through the counter-high tables covered with skeins of yarn, and under the tables, the cubbies overflowed. Two walls held boxes of even more yarn, and on one wall was a rack of pattern books and other accessories: needles, hooks, and gadgets whose purpose I didn't understand. "This shop is a rainbow of color and texture."

Beth laughed as she entered the room. "This from the designer whose workroom looks very similar."

"I guess we're alike." I flashed her a smile, glad she wasn't still upset about my comment accusing Amos of being a dirty cop. However, my two conversations this morning convinced me more than ever that something was up with him, and it wasn't his height.

"I saw muffins on the counter. Goodies from Brewed Bliss?"

With a laugh, I said, "You don't want me to bake. But yes, I took your suggestion and stopped in after I went to Twice Loved. I met Fiona. She's lovely."

Ethan said, "If you'd like, I'll stop at the shop and hang the bell."

"Great. I don't have any tools yet, but I would like to have it in place, especially since people seem to drop by whenever they want."

He said, "People in town are excited to see life in the store again. Herman was well liked."

"As I'm slowly meeting other shop owners, I'm discovering that." I took a cup of coffee and added the cream and sugar. What the heck? I might as well broach the topic of Amos again. "I bumped into Barbara and Amos outside the coffee shop. She was crying."

Beth paused mid-stir. "Really? I didn't know they were speaking. It was a nasty breakup when she started dating Knox. I'm sure he was convinced it would be them against the world forever." She took a sunshine muffin and a napkin, and I did the same.

"She really broke it off because Amos lacked money?" I sipped my coffee while keeping an eye on Beth's face.

"Yeah. In my book, that's not real love."

"Mine, either. It doesn't seem like Sue or Fiona are fans of Amos. Does he annoy everyone in town?"

Ethan said, "He rubs people the wrong way. I've been thinking about what you mentioned regarding him coming to the store and giving you that card. Please let me know immediately if it happens again or he tries anything unethical."

"I will." At least that backed up what Sue had said about reaching out to Ethan. I wouldn't feel comfortable calling the station to report Amos.

"Are the cameras working well?" he asked.

"Yes, and this morning, when I checked the videos overnight, it was quiet except for the wind and a few seagulls."

"At this time of year, the winds are wicked off the bay, but you'll be happy for them come summer. There's nothing like a breeze on your upper deck come mid-July."

Beth laughed, "And I'll be sitting next to you. My tiny back entrance doesn't have the view or the breeze."

"Anytime. You know that."

Beth said, "We should relax and enjoy the quiet before the day gets busy." She guided me to the upholstered chairs in the back corner. Ethan took his coffee into the other room.

"I can tell something's bothering you. Care to share, or do I need to drag it out of you?"

I glanced at my cup. "I'm not sure it makes a difference now that Prescott's dead."

"Why?" She set her cup aside and turned to me.

"When I spoke with Fiona, she said Prescott wanted to buy Grants Gowns, Twice Loved, and Whistlers Inn to create a huge motel."

She nodded. "Ah, that makes total sense, but he would have had difficulty getting it approved by the board unless he kept it within a certain size and appearance. We have strict ordinances in town regarding new construction. But that would be a cash cow if it were approved." She broke the muffin in half and took a bite.

"I'm confused. If Prescott and Herman argued and he fell down the stairs and died, why would someone want to kill Prescott?" I couldn't tell her that Herman remembered it was Amos in his apartment. Getting information from a ghost was helpful and problematic at the same time. I brushed crumbs from my fingertips. That was one delish muffin.

"The two deaths must not be related."

Ethan came in, and Beth said, "Dad, did you hear anything about a new motel replacing the inn, Fiona's place, and Claudia's?"

"I heard a rumor. Some developers have been sniffing around a couple of times, but it's nothing the board would approve. Why do you ask?"

"Fiona said Prescott wanted to buy all the bayside properties. He had a grand plan."

"One that would have fallen short." Ethan took the box he was carrying to the racks. "At least you won't have that to deal with any longer."

"True. Do you think the cops will solve Herman's death?" When they did, I was sure that meant his ghost would leave.

"The case will remain open until we understand for certain what happened. It's the same with Colton Prescott. Even though the leads are sketchy at this point, we have to trust the process. It's just a matter of time."

"Dad, did anything come back on the gun found at the scene of Prescott's murder?"

He concentrated on stacking books on the rack, and Beth nodded and held up her hand, indicating patience. It was crazy how I already understood her different looks and reactions—but in a good way.

He stopped what he was doing and crossed the room. "I'm not supposed to say anything, and I'd appreciate it if you don't repeat a word outside of this room, but the gun that was found at the scene wasn't the murder weapon. It was Prescott's gun. My theory; he had it for self-protection and never got to use it when he was threatened. Bullets were in all five chambers."

"That means me picking it up is irrelevant to the investigation." My insides tightened. I wished the murder weapon would at least be out of circulation.

"Another reason Amos shouldn't bug you about being the primary suspect. Although they still don't have anyone they're zeroing in on."

"Any word on what kind of gun was used?" Beth asked.

"The most common handgun in the United States, a 9mm Glock."

"That doesn't narrow it down. Even I have one of those."

I looked at Beth. "You own a gun?"

"Yes, it's pretty common around here. I like to hike and I take a handgun with me for protection against wildlife."

I had never considered that a reason to carry a gun, but it made sense. I drained the last of my coffee. "I've procrastinated long enough and have to get back to work but this was a nice interlude. It's time to roll up my sleeves and dive into the chaos of my workroom." I stood and waited for Beth to hand me her now-empty cup. "Thanks for allowing me a place to escape for a little while."

She laughed. "Any time. Do you want help later? I can be free," she glanced at her phone, "say around two?"

"You're welcome to come over if you want to keep me company, but you don't need to work." I gestured to her winter white slacks and lavender Fair Isle knit sweater. "That's a chatting outfit, not one for scrubbing." I pulled on my coat and hat, then wound the scarf around my neck.

Giving me a playful poke in the shoulder, she said, "Good thing I live upstairs. I can change my clothes on a whim."

"There's no need. But stop over anytime."

Ethan said, "Let me get my coat and drill. I'll walk over with you, and we can install the bell in a couple of minutes."

"Are you sure? It can wait."

"Not at all. Why put it off until later when I can do it now?" He pointed to the box he had been emptying. "I'll finish that when I get back. Someone needs a pair of mittens."

I put my hands behind my back and whistled tunelessly.

"That's good thinking, Dad. I just need to bind off. I'll bring them over later. You'll get frostbite if you don't start wearing something on your hands."

Tapping my fingertips to my palms, I said, "They're tough from all the hand sewing I've done for years. Besides, spring is right around the corner." I pointed to the front window. "That little yellow orb in the sky is warming the earth as we speak."

"Nice try, Claudia. I'll see you later. Thanks for the muffins and coffee."

"My pleasure." I took the paper bag from the counter. "My bell."

Ethan and I jogged across the street using the crosswalk as I held the neck of my coat close to my scarf. Dang, it was cold. I slipped the key into the front door lock and pushed it open. Warmth washed over us. I was glad I remembered to turn the heat up earlier. "Come in."

He closed the door and flipped the lock. "Do you have a step stool?"

"In the back room." I slipped off my coat, tossed it on a sofa, and toed off my heavy boots. There was no sense in tracking dirt over the carpet. I entered the workroom but remembered I had taken it upstairs to put some shoe boxes in the top of my closet. Poking my head around the corner, I said, "Ethan, it's upstairs. I'll be right back."

"I can get it."

"It'll only take a sec." I turned on the stairwell light and dashed up, my socks muffling my steps.

Herman perched on the window ledge. "How was your morning?"

"Great. I met Fiona and Sue, and there's a lot to share, but Ethan's downstairs installing a new bell over the door. We can talk after he leaves."

"I'm not going anywhere."

I slid on my socks down the hall like a kid, feeling lighter than I had since discovering what had happened to Herman. Everything was going to be okay. I folded the stool, headed for the stairs, and noticed my dry-erase board shoved against the wall. *That wasn't where I had left it.*

"Herman, was someone here?" But he had disappeared. "I'll ask Ethan to look around with me before he goes."

Taking care not to trip, I navigated the steps. Stopping when I heard a thud and then a groan. It sounded like someone had toppled onto the floor.

"Ethan?" I crept around the corner. Amos was standing next to Ethan's lifeless body. "What happened?" I ran to him and dropped to my knees.

20

———

mos said, "I was walking past the shop when Ethan waved me inside. The minute I closed the door, he grunted and slumped to the floor."

I touched his wrist and felt the steady thrum under my fingertips. "Call 9-1-1 and ask for an ambulance. He might be having a heart attack."

"He'll be okay, and he doesn't have a history of heart issues."

Lifting his head, I felt something warm and sticky on my fingers. I knew without looking what I'd find.

"Maybe we should have a chat before Ethan wakes up." Amos bobbed his head to a sofa.

I stood slowly, leaning him against the door. Smears of red over the white paint would surely be an attention-getter if something went wrong. Attention, that's what I needed.

"Give me a moment." I took several deep breaths, waiting for Amos to roll his eyes or do anything indicating annoyance. Then, I pretended to stumble against the wall and flipped the outside light switch and prayed Beth would remember my distress signal.

"Get over there. We need to talk." He yanked my arm,

careful not to get my hands close to his jacket. It wouldn't do to have blood on his uniform.

I hesitated. "Can I at least prop Ethan up better? It might help slow down blood loss." I had no idea if this was true, but it was worth a shot.

He tapped his nightstick against his thigh. "Be quick about it."

I eased Ethan away from the door, and checked to see if the lock was turned; it wasn't. Given the circumstances, the only thing I could do was to prop him into a sitting position against a wooden chair.

"Are you finished?" Amos asked.

Herman zipped into the room and hovered beside Ethan. "What happened?"

"You didn't have to knock him out." I glared at Ethan.

"I didn't." He nodded over his shoulder. Barbara hovered in the corner, smiling at him, she crossed the room.

"It was me. I didn't mean to hurt him, but in my defense, he startled me."

"What are you doing in my shop?" I rose to my feet, putting myself as a shield between Ethan and Amos and Barbara.

Herman took his place by my side. "If you can get to my desk, on the left between it and the file cabinet, is a baseball bat—an old wooden slugger. With the correct swing, you can disable one and get the chance to run."

That was good information, but at the moment, they stood between me and the bat. I cocked a brow. "Why are you here, looking to get a jump on the spring line?"

"No. But I am looking for something special, my charm. Amos lost it when he and Herman were having a disagreement. I want it back. It's all I have left of our time together." Her eyes got misty when she looked at him.

"What charm?"

"Remember I told you he bought one with two halves as a promise to me?"

"I haven't seen anything." I thought of the half of a charm Eddie had taken with him to compare and confirm that it matched the charm discovered in Prescott's hand.

"Can't you be satisfied with the other half as a memento?"

"Well, that's sort of the issue." She dropped her chin and looked at me through lowered lashes. "I lost mine, too. If I could find one half, it would comfort me."

"You have a new life. Aren't you a newlywed?" I inched my way around Barbara. I needed to get to the desk. I couldn't take two of them down with one swing but I sure as heck wouldn't stand here defenseless.

"I want my charm." Her words cracked like a bolt of lightning.

I froze. It took several deep breaths before I said, "I don't have it. But we can look for it. What was it?"

"Stop playing dumb. A half of a four-leaf clover. Why don't you remember our conversation?"

"Wait a minute. You said Amos dropped it during a disagreement with Herman. When?" My gaze slid from her to him.

His face flushed crimson. "The day he died."

"You were here? I thought Colton Prescott pushed Herman."

With wide eyes, he said, "Why do you think he was pushed?"

"Educated guess. Ethan mentioned he was found at the bottom of the stairs. Since this had been his home for years, it's an assumption he could navigate them in his sleep. But what were you doing here?"

"Herman had a recording of a conversation we had. I wanted it back."

"I haven't found any tapes."

He grinned. "That's because recently I learned he was bluffing."

"You pushed an elderly man down a flight of stairs over a conversation?" My hands formed fists at my sides. I wanted to pummel him, but he towered over me. "And how do you know the tape doesn't exist?"

"It wasn't a simple conversation. He was stupid enough to say he recorded us discussing his lack of payments to the protection fund. I've searched every inch of this building; there's no tape recorder or tape. Ergo, he was bluffing. For the record, I didn't push him. He fell."

"And you didn't call for help?"

Amos lifted a shoulder. "How could I explain what I was doing here? I searched the place, but Ethan came through the front, I slipped out the back. It took months of searching before I realized it was a ruse. You might have contributed to my luck since you arrived and tidied the place. It was easier to finish my search."

"You ignored his injuries?" I shook my fist at him. "You're responsible for his death."

Barbara took a menacing step toward me. "If Herman had just paid his dues, he'd be alive and well today. Besides, Amos just told me he lost his half of the charm, and I'm sure it has to be here. So, where is it?"

I continued to slide at a snail's pace toward the workroom door. "What day did you come to your conclusion?"

"Wednesday."

Clues were clicking into place. "Those were your boot prints outside my back door?"

"Yeah, I knew from Prescott that you were meeting that morning. As soon as you left, I wandered in. But I couldn't find the charm."

"Did you call me to confirm the meeting?"

Barbara laughed. "No. I did. I'm pretty good at imitating

the old coot's voice, don't you agree? All I did was cover the phone with a scarf, talk deeper, and you fell for it."

"Barbara shut up. If you keep spilling your guts, Claudia must have an accident."

A shiver snaked down my spine. But before I made my move, I had to know. "Amos, why did you shoot Prescott?"

"I'm not a cold-blooded killer, even though that's the direction your murder board was leaning. However, I'll admit to having another slight disagreement with the man. It turns out he's been watching me. Cunning busybody. He overheard my conversations with others and put two and two together. That night I confronted him, and he threatened to expose my side hustle. Barbara saw my truck outside of Prescott's and was eavesdropping."

"Seems a lot of that happens around town." I didn't care that my comment was snide. These people were ticking me off. "Was Prescott alive when you left him?"

"Well, not exactly." He took Barbara's hand. "Deep emotions can make a woman act impulsively. My love snuck into the house from the back door and waited until Prescott entered his office."

She placed her hand on his arm. "I had to protect Amos. If I was going to leave my marriage, I had to ensure he'd be able to provide for me. If anyone could persuade Colton to forget what he knew, it would be me. After all, I've never met a man I couldn't convince to see things my way. Unfortunately, we struggled, and he grabbed my necklace."

"The one with the half of a charm?" I couldn't believe what I was hearing.

She tipped her chin up. "Yes. During the tussle, the gun went off. He slumped to the floor. It was an accident, but Amos heard the shot and rushed in to find me standing over Prescott."

He was shaking his head and pressed his fingers to his eyes.

"You shouldn't have confessed. I spent a lot of time covering up any evidence you were in that house. Now," he bobbed his head in my direction, "I'll have to make this problem disappear."

"Snookums." Barbara put her arms around his waist and lay her head on his chest.

Finally, this was my chance.

Herman said, "Come on."

As quietly as possible, I slipped into the other room, following Herman's fleeting shape.

"Here." He hovered on the left side of the desk. My fingers curled around the smooth wooden cylinder. I was going down swinging. Creeping back to the door, Herman nodded.

Barbara looked at me from the safety of Amos's arms and laughed. "Do you think you can take us down? It's two against one."

Ethan was struggling to get to his knees. He put a finger to his lips. I stayed focused on the killers standing in front of me. "You have two choices. Turn yourselves into the police and confess to what you've done, or I'll make sure you are held responsible."

Amos laughed. "You're going to assault an officer of the law with a bat. You can get jail time for that. Besides, I can tweak the evidence in the Prescott murder. You'll be spending a lot of time in orange."

Barbara laughed. "Based on your coloring, that won't suit you at all." She lunged for me.

I swung as hard as I could, connecting across her midsection. She crumpled to the floor. Amos charged as Ethan reached out and grabbed him by the ankle, causing him to land face-first at my feet.

The door to the shop burst open. Three officers and Eddie burst in, guns drawn. "Everybody freeze!"

I dropped the bat to the floor and thrust my arms in the

air. "Don't shoot." I pointed a finger at Barbara and Amos. "They were going to kill me, and she assaulted Ethan."

"Um. Any chance you can call the EMTs." He gingerly touched the back of his head and winced. "I might need a couple of stitches."

Outside, Beth paced the sidewalk. Her arms wrapped around her as she moved from side to side, attempting to glimpse what was happening.

"Eddie, can I help Ethan?"

He nodded and stood over the couple. "Amos Branson and Barbara Hall, you're under arrest." He glanced at me and mouthed, *For?*

"Barbara killed Colton Prescott, and Amos is responsible for Herman's death. Also, he's behind the break-ins here."

He lifted his head. "I didn't kill him. He fell."

"And you left him to die so that you could find a stupid tape that didn't exist." Hot tears burned my eyes as I sank to the floor beside Ethan.

"Eddie, are you gonna believe her over people you've known your entire life?"

Ethan said, "I heard the confession and got it on my cell." He slumped against my shoulder. Whispering, he said, "Herman would have been so proud. You're fearless."

Beth dashed through the door. "Dad. Claudia."

Ethan held out his hand. "I'll be fine, kiddo. Just a bump on the head."

She clutched our hands, heedless of the blood on them, hers warm against my icy fingers. "I don't know how I can ever thank you for saving my dad."

Eddie waited until Amos and Barbara were in handcuffs before lowering his gun. He took my hand and pulled me up. "We should give the professionals space to process the scene, and I need to take your statement."

"First, can I ask a question?"

He nodded.

"Did the charm half I gave you match what you found in Prescott's hand?"

"Perfectly. Was it Barbara's?"

I watched the police lead them from my store to the waiting police cruisers. "Yes. It's sad. Money and love ended two lives and almost destroyed so many more."

He embraced me tightly. For my ears alone, he said, "Thanks for saving Ethan. We were aware of the extortion; I've been working on the case for months."

I gave him a small smile. "Look at that: three investigations were closed today." I surveyed the room but didn't see Herman's translucent form anywhere. I wished I had gotten a chance to say goodbye and thank him.

The shop was unnaturally silent after the EMTs left with Ethan and Beth. She promised to call as soon as they were home from the hospital. The police finished collecting evidence of Amos and Barbara's break in, and Eddie checked the locks to make sure they were working correctly before he left. I curled up on the sofa with Lola in my lap.

I ran my fingers through her long fur and waited for Herman to drift in.

My cell rang. "Hello."

"It's Beth. I wanted to let you know Dad told me everything while waiting for the doctor. Lady, you've got nerves of titanium. Grilling those two took guts, and he said your first concern was for him." A sob broke her words. "Thank you."

"Beth, it's my fault he was attacked." My gut twisted when I wondered what they would have done to him. "If he hadn't been helping me, he wouldn't have gotten caught up in the mess."

"But we might have lost you."

I fell silent. What she said was true. Amos never actually pulled the trigger, but he might not have stopped Barbara if she had wanted to shoot me. The only saving grace was that if she had used the same gun, the evidence would show it wasn't my choice to leave this earth, and the guilty person would now be responsible for two deaths.

"Claudia, are you still there?"

"Yes. Sorry. My thoughts ran away with me."

"I was asking you to come over to my place tonight. Dad will stay with me for a few days, and Eddie has a few off-the-record questions."

"It's been a long week, and I don't think that's a great idea."

"I'm not taking no for an answer. Besides, I have your mittens finished. Eddie will swing by your place around six and walk with you."

Before I could protest, she hung up. "Lola, I'm going to Beth's for dinner. Maybe I should try baking a box of brownies or something."

She yawned, stretched her paws to my cheeks, and gently patted them.

"Don't worry, little fluff ball, we're in this life together."

Gathered around Beth's dining table, Eddie poured me another glass of wine. "What a day."

I nodded and gave him a small smile. "You aren't just-a-kidding."

He wrinkled his brow.

"Sorry, an old expression from my grandfather."

"It's quaint." He poured wine into his glass. "Do you mind if we debrief the case?"

"If you'd like, but as you know I've already made a statement."

"I know, humor me? I knew Amos was tied up in this somehow. At Prescott's, he was acting odd. I didn't know how exactly until I found him in the shop. Then I realized he had been coming and going since Herman died."

I twirled the wine in my glass. "And the charm? How did that play into the equation?"

Eddie said, "If I had known the charm was Barbara's, it would have been logical to realize they were messed up with something, but I never guessed she shot Prescott."

Beth nodded encouraging me to keep talking.

"At first, when Amos said he was waiting for me to leave the shop, I thought he killed Prescott earlier in the day. That's why he was first on the scene. Since he knew about the shooting, he needed to make sure I was implicated. If you remember, he jumped to that conclusion immediately. One thing he hadn't counted on was Prescott's gun. He didn't realize they were different calibers. He put it together and realized Barbara's gun would need to be disposed of. If things went as planned, my guess is I would have been shot with her gun, and it was left with my body. All tidy, with them getting away with murder."

He wiped a hand over his face and looked at Ethan. "Too bad Claudia's a dress designer. We could use someone like her on the force." He looked at me. "You've got great instincts."

I winked at Beth. "Not bad for sofa sleuths."

Ethan grinned, and Beth said, "I'm glad you came up with the outside light-on signal."

"Me, too." I shuddered.

"As soon as I noticed it, I called Dad, and when he didn't answer, Eddie was my next phone call."

"Did Barbara think she and Amos would ride off into the sunset together after she divorced her husband?" I asked.

Beth lifted a shoulder. "Apparently. Knox will file for the divorce and wash his hands of her."

"Maybe I should make her a custom-designed jumpsuit."

Ethan snorted. "After all, orange might be her best color."

I looked around the table at my new friends. "Murder

mysteries notwithstanding, you three are terrific. Moving to Drakes Bay might have been my best decision in a long time."

Eddie said, "Now the town can return to its sleepy status, and the sofa sleuths can hang up their magnifying glasses."

Beth winked at me. "Cousin, you wish."

My face broke into a wide smile. "You said I had a knack for investigating. We'll have to improve our skills in case you need our help again."

Ethan and Eddie shook their heads.

Eddie said, "Maybe you and Beth should concentrate on running your businesses and let me do police work."

I leaned back in my chair. "We'll see. But there is still one mystery, the possible combination to the safe."

Eddie said, "We can try it if you want, run over and then come back and share the news?"

I nodded and stood. "Let's."

We jogged across the street and in through the front, down the basement stairs, clicking on lights. My heart hammered in my chest. The final piece of the puzzle.

I walked into the fabric room and moved the leather. Eddie hovered at my elbow. "This is exciting."

I glanced his way and grinned. I tapped the keys with the numbers I had memorized, and the door sprung open. Laying inside was a piece of paper. I withdrew it. *New safe for Claudia.*

Eddie's eyes widened and I laughed. "So much for a mystery or great treasure."

August

I peeked through the window and breathed a sigh of relief when two women, Lily Michaels and Nikki Twing, got out of an SUV. Standing in the center of the main salon, I waited for them to close the door. My stomach tumbled and I pressed a hand over my midsection to quell the queasiness and smoothed my hand over my hair. These were my first customers, picking up Gigi Originals; well, tweaks from Herman's designs—but it counted.

"Lily, Nikki, welcome. I put your gowns in the dressing rooms. Who's going first?"

Lily looked at Nikki. "She is."

I whisked Nikki into the next room, closed the door, and gestured to the gown hanging on the hook. "Do you need help?"

"I'm all set. You'd better check on the bride. She's been a bundle of nerves this morning."

"Of course."

Lily was moving around the space when I entered the room, her fingers trailing over dress fabrics. She peered closely at the intricate lace work on one gown. "This is beautiful."

I folded the swatch back against a dark velvet piece to highlight the pattern, "I found it in my Great-Uncle Herman's workroom. He either created it or purchased it and never used it. I thought it needed to be on a dress."

She nodded. "It's beautiful." A light breeze slid over my arm, as if the window were open or it was a ghost. Rumor had it Lily was a witch. Could she see or sense other spirits?

"Nikki will be out shortly, if you want to take a seat." I gestured toward an upholstered chair.

Lily sat and crossed her legs, turning her head toward the lacy curtains that fluttered at the closed window.

I stepped in front of her. "Here's Nikki."

She floated in, stopped before us, and made a slow turn. "Well, what do you think?"

The sage green chiffon dress was perfect, from the sweetheart neckline to the sweep of the cascading skirt. Lily placed a hand over her heart as her face softened. "Nikki, you're stunning."

She took Lily's hand, beaming. "Put your dress on, and we'll stand side by side."

I knew they would look perfect. Lily and I entered the next dressing room, where her gown hung on a padded hanger.

Lily slipped from her outfit and stepped into the draping fabric, and I zipped the A-line chiffon white dress. The embellished sleeveless V-neck bodice, adorned with white pearls and quartz crystals swept into a floor-length skirt with a train. She wore an amethyst and black tourmaline necklace.

With a snap of my fingers, I smiled. "I have the perfect pair of earrings to go with your necklace, if that's what you'll wear at the wedding."

"I never take it off. I'd love to see them."

I slipped quietly from the room as Lily gazed into the mirror.

When I returned, she was finger-combing her hair. "That style is perfect with your gown." I handed her a pair of chandelier earrings featuring three stones: black tourmaline was the first stone, with two oval amethyst stones cascading in silver filigree. She held them to her ears and looked in the mirror. "They match perfectly."

"Try them on. They can be your something borrowed."

She secured them to her ear lobes, and her eyes widened before returning to normal. "Are these yours?"

"They are, and I'm happy to loan them to you."

"I'd like that." She looked in the mirror again. She was a stunning bride.

"Are you ready to show Nikki?"

Wiping her cheek with the back of her hand, she smiled. "Thank you, Claudia. I wasn't planning to put the dress on, but I'm glad I did. I can't believe I'll be a bride in less than a week."

"And a beautiful one at that." I gave her a quick hug,

careful not to crush the dress. "You still have your reception dress to try on, too."

She fanned herself with her hand and giggled. "I'm not sure I can take the excitement."

Nikki tapped on the door. "Lily, if you're not coming out, I'm coming in."

She eased the door open and sashayed into the main room. Holding her arms out, she gave a slow spin. "Well, what do you think?"

Nikki clapped her hands together and sighed. "Oh, Lily. You were meant to be a bride. The gown is perfect, and when Gage sees you, his heart will stop beating."

"I certainly hope not." She slipped her arm around Nikki's waist, and they stood, gazing into the mirror. "Every day of my life has led me to this point."

Nikki nodded and sniffed. "You and Gage are meant to be together. If nothing else, the events of the last couple of years prove that."

My brow creased, curious to know what that meant, but I maintained my cool demeanor.

Lily shrugged. "With Nikki and a few friends, we've helped Gage solve a few murders in town."

She scoffed. "A few. We've had eleven; without Lily's help, some might have gotten away with it."

I felt my eyes bug wide. It sounded familiar to what Beth and I did a few months ago. "Sounds scary." A crash from the back room drew my attention. "I'm sorry. Would you excuse me for a minute?"

"Sure. I'll put the other dress on."

I rushed into the back room, but it was empty. *Herman!*

I rushed back to the salon so the ladies could complete their fittings. An hour later, I closed the front door as two satisfied customers pulled away from the curb. Alone, I placed my hands on my hips. "Herman, come out here right now!"

. . .

If you loved Ghosts & Gowns, help other readers find this book:
Please leave a review now!
Are you ready to read more from the Lily and the gang in Pembroke?
Keep reading for a sneak peek at
Buttons & Burglary
A Craft and Ghost Cozy Mystery
A Dress Designer Cozy Mystery Series
Order Now
Or
Shop at Lucinda Race

Lucinda

I hope you want to keep up with my crazy antics of writing, gardening, cooking, and life with the pups.

Not ready to stop reading yet? If you sign up for my newsletter at www.lucindarace.com/newsletter, you will receive an excerpt for Cookies & Capers, the introduction of when Lily met Milo right away, as my thank-you gift for choosing to get my newsletter.

Buttons & Burglary
Enjoy this humorous, small-town, psychic, cozy mystery by best-selling and award-winning Lucinda Race.

Thread carefully—a fashionable pair of sofa sleuths unbutton a mystery that could cost them everything.

Burglary, She Buttoned

Fashion designer Claudia Grant is finally feeling at home in Drakes Bay. Her dress shop is thriving, her monthly dinners with vintage-loving Fiona Doyle are a cozy highlight—and she's even grown used to sharing the space with her ghostly Uncle Herman. But when a bride-to-be brings in a vintage wedding dress missing its buttons, Claudia turns to Fiona, who always seems to have just the right antique treasure.

Only this time, the treasure comes at a potentially deadly cost. When Claudia arrives for their Sunday night supper, dessert in hand, she finds Fiona unconscious—and the box of buttons she'd promised to show her, has been stolen. With the police short on leads, Claudia and her best friend, Beth, decide to unravel the mystery themselves, stitch by stitch.

In a town where secrets are as well-kept as heirloom lace, can Claudia thread the needle before the thief turns violent again?

Buttons & Burglary
A Craft and Ghost Cozy Mystery
Order Now

LUCINDA RACE

Buttons & and Burglary

A CRAFT AND GHOST COZY MYSTERY
A DRESS DESIGNER COZY MYSTERY SERIES
BOOK TWO

CHAPTER ONE

I settled into a deck chair savoring the warm afternoon, the view of Drakes Bay, and a glass of lemonade on the side table. Then my cell phone pinged. It was Beth, the owner of Knit or Purl and my new best friend.

Be over in ten. Bringing appetizers.

I grinned. Dinner alfresco sounded perfect after the day I'd had. One issue after another arose, not with my brides but with their mothers. It was time to put the day behind me. I glanced at my watch and saw I still had time to call about the antique buttons. Twice Loved, the second-hand shop in town, was open. I dialed and waited for Fiona Doyle to answer.

"Hello, Twice Loved."

"Hi, Fiona. It's Claudia Grant."

"Hello. This is a surprise. I didn't expect to hear from you until Sunday. You're still coming for dinner, aren't you?"

"I'm looking forward to it." It had been a standing monthly invitation that my late Uncle Herman and Fiona had. When I first moved to town and discovered his ghost was lingering, he asked if I'd continue to have dinner with his old friend.

"Excellent. What can I do for you tonight?"

"I worked with a bride today. She asked me to refresh her grandmother's wedding dress, which was missing buttons. I hoped to look through your button boxes to see if I could find some that would match or at least complement the dress."

"Of course. Recently, I purchased a box at an auction. If you'd like to come over now, I can unpack it. I don't mind staying open a little later."

"No, thank you. I don't want you to go to any trouble tonight, but if I could look on Sunday, that would give me plenty of time to devise a new plan if nothing would work."

"Absolutely. I'll check to make sure I don't have any other boxes tucked away. Sometimes, I squirrel away fun do-dads to peruse on a rainy day."

"Great." Now that business was settled, I asked, "Would you like me to bring anything special for dessert on Sunday?"

"Whatever you'd like." She giggled like a schoolgirl. "I've never met a sweet I didn't enjoy."

"Then it will be a surprise."

"Goodbye, Claudia. See you soon, and don't forget to come hungry."

She disconnected, and I smiled. Herman had been right when he said Fiona was wonderful. Personally, I think he had a crush on the woman and was too shy to speak up. But that ship sailed.

I went inside my apartment. "Lola, time for dinner." The sweet Himalayan cat thumped into the kitchen and jumped on the table. She stared at me.

"Did I interrupt your nap, little lady?" A breeze slid over my arm. "Herman. You've made yourself scarce today."

"That woman, the bride's mother, Mrs. Vanderkemp, is insufferable. I couldn't listen to another minute of her moaning about remaking that hideous dress—her words, not mine."

"Julia is sweet, and the dress isn't that bad, despite what her mother thinks." He was right. I didn't have a bridezilla on my hands; I had a MOB-zilla. "It'll be beautiful when I'm done with it."

"I'm sure it will. You're quite talented, but the best part of being a ghost is that I no longer have to deal with customers like her."

I laughed. "You're a resident ghost with strong opinions. How did I get so lucky?"

He frowned. "I should have crossed over to where I'm meant to live for eternity after you found out how I died. I believe you're stuck with me forever."

"There are worse fates than hanging out with me." I opened a can of food for Lola and set the plate on the table, giving her ears a quick scratch. I had given up trying to convince her that cats ate their food on the floor. A good scrub of the table was all that was needed when she was finished. At least she didn't get on the table all the time, just for meals.

"You're right. Don't you wonder why I'm still here?"

"Unfinished business, I suppose." I poured a glass of lemonade for Beth and placed it on a tray with small plates and napkins.

If a ghost could sigh, Herman did before he drifted from the kitchen. I knew he would take his usual spot on the window ledge in the living room, look down the street, or make his way to the dress shop.

I was about to comfort him when I heard Beth call to me.

"Claudia, are you coming out?"

I picked up the tray and walked to the door. Pushing the screen with my hip, I stepped onto the deck. "Your timing is perfect. I've fed Lola, and it's time to put our feet up."

She placed a tray overfilled with finger foods on the table between the lounge chairs and reclined. "It's been a day. Is there a full moon tonight? I swear every customer was out to push my buttons."

"Same." I set my tray on the dining table and passed her the lemonade, plate, and a napkin. "I had a MOB-zilla."

She wrinkled her nose. "What's that?"

"A mother of the bride who's acting like Godzilla."

"I get it now. Someone local?"

I eased into the chair after filling a small plate. "No, that's the funny part. They're from New Hampshire. I never thought anyone would drive a long distance to my little dress shop. Despite that, the mother of the bride is lovely, and I can't wait to design dresses for the two attendants."

"You possess a unique talent for making people feel beautiful when they wear one of your designs. It's truly a special gift."

Heat flushed my cheeks. "Thank you. I— I don't know what to say."

She held up her glass. "Cheers to us. We survived our customers and a long day. Tomorrow will be easier."

With a laugh, our glasses clinked together. "Salute."

I leaned back. "I can't believe it's been six months since I moved to Drakes Bay. Living in Maine is a dream come true."

"After the rocky start, the sofa sleuths started strong, but since we solved the murder of Colton Prescott and Herman's death, life's returned to normal. Well, except for the summer tourists."

"I think we should leave solving crimes to your cousin, Eddie." I sipped my drink, hoping to avoid her questioning look. I tried hard not to show anyone that I thought he was the best thing since the invention of the sewing machine and oh-so sigh-worthy.

"He's not dating anyone. Why don't you ask him out? The fall festival in Pembroke Cove is coming up soon."

"I have too much that requires my attention. The business is more than a full-time job."

She snorted. "Right. We could go to the festival if you want. It's a lot of fun; you'll see Lily and Gage again. She always has a booth with her parents' tea for sale."

"That sounds like fun."

With a saucy wink, she said, "I'll ask Eddie to come with us. Just as a friend for you, of course."

I shook my head. Eager to change the subject, I cleared my throat. "The dress I'm going to remake is missing some buttons. Do you have anything in your shop that could be considered antique knockoffs?"

"Stop in before we open tomorrow, and I'll let you look around. But Fiona's store would be a better option."

"She mentioned that I could view her inventory on Sunday when I'm there for dinner. However, I don't have high hopes of finding what I need. Having a backup plan could help me avoid a trip to Boston or New York City. I'm sure I could find what I'd like there, but I'd prefer not to waste the time driving."

"I have button books available for you to check out, and ordering through me can help you save money. What about your inventory?"

"Nothing will work. I've already checked the basement where Herman kept old lace and leather. He didn't collect buttons."

We nibbled in silence.

"Herman was a terrific guy. I wish you could have met him."

I spoke to his ghost every day and likely knew him as well as I would have if he were alive. "I feel like I know him after everything you and your dad have shared. Fiona's filled in some gaps, too."

"That's good." She pulled out her phone. "Hold on, it's Eddie." She pressed a button on her cell. "Hey, cuz, what's up?" With a nod, she smiled. "We were just talking about that." Pause. "I'll ask her and get back to you, but it sounds great." Another pause. "Talk soon." She grinned. "You'll never guess what Eddie wanted."

With a chuckle, I said, "You can tell me, and we'll both know."

"Eddie asked if we wanted to go with him and Luke Devlin to the Pembroke Cove Fall Festival next Saturday."

"Did you set this up?"

She waved a hand at me. "Innocent. But this indicates that Eddie wants a reason to spend time with you, and Luke is adorable." With a wink, she laughed. "I can endure his company for an afternoon."

"Sounds more like a date for you two and we're making plans ten days in advance?"

"Correct. It will give us plenty of time to find something to wear."

"I'm guessing both guys know what you look like, and Eddie has spent time around me, so why go through all the trouble of picking outfits?"

"Well, if Eddie doesn't trip your trigger, then maybe you'll meet someone else, so you need to look nice. But I'm sure he's got a thing for you."

I shook my head. "I try to always look decent."

She patted my arm. "Claudia, you wear black or navy almost every day while working. It's time to put a lot of color in your wardrobe."

"I have color." My thoughts drifted to my closet, and she was right; most of it was monochromatic. But I had nine days to whip up a new top that I could pair with jeans.

"It might be cool, so you'll want a nice sweater. I have the perfect one at the store. I finished it last night and planned to wear it, but you can try it first."

"You're determined to increase the contents in my sweater drawer."

"If we continue to support each other with our talents, we'll have the best wardrobes in town."

"And we'll be walking advertisements for our stores." I raised my hand for a high five.

"Women businesses working together is our superpower."

"It is." Darkness crept across the bay. "I know I haven't

told you, but I'm happy we're friends. You made the transition much easier."

"I know what you mean." She clasped my hand. "Even if we never have to be sofa sleuths again, we've got each other's backs in every aspect of life, and I'm fortunate you moved to town. Making good friends has been difficult for me. The girls at school thought I was odd growing up because I loved to knit."

I understood exactly what she meant. "Sewing wasn't exactly popular, either."

Getting to her feet, Beth stretched her arms over her head. "Look at us now. Forging our destinies with amazing businesses in a charming coastal town. What more could we ask for in life?"

I couldn't think of anything. "Antique buttons?" I chuckled. "If that's my biggest challenge this week, aside from MOB-zilla, I'm a happy seamstress."

It was nine the next morning when I crossed the street to Knit or Purl. The door was propped open, and I went in. "Beth?"

I heard a muffled response that sounded like "In the office."

Wandering through the yarn shop had become a favorite pastime. I hesitated but contemplated picking up a beginner set of needles and yarn. Every set was designed for children, but my foolish pride held me back each time.

"Morning." Beth emerged from the back room, holding several magazines. "I brought my accessory catalogs for you to take with you." She set them on the counter. "First, let's look at a few options on the rack."

I walked with her as she guided me to the back wall. "You never said if the buttons were covered, metal, or wood."

"The buttons might have been ivory colored or pearl and secured with a loop, so there are no buttonholes."

She nodded. "Then what I have here won't work. I don't

have any ivory buttons in stock. I thought maybe there were covered buttons, and I do have that option, since I've used them as a base for crocheted buttons."

"Is there any end to your talent with yarn?"

She laughed. "I hope not. I keep pushing myself to learn new techniques and styles."

I scanned the rack, but nothing caught my eye. "I'll take the books. After I look at Fiona's stock, I'll figure out my next step."

"Just tell me how I can help."

The door opened. The bell above it jingled as Ethan walked in. "Good morning, ladies."

"Hi, Dad. Did you stop at Brewed Bliss?"

He held up a paper bag and cardboard tray. "As requested." His smile grew. "Good morning, Claudia."

"Hi, Ethan. How's things?"

"Good. I just chatted with Chief Durgin, and he mentioned that Barbara Hall and Amos Branson took a plea deal, and he wanted me to pass along his thanks for the details you provided."

"That took a long time." I took the coffee he held out to me.

"Not really. It takes time to bring people to trial, and during the waiting period, I think Barbara and Amos thought about what happened and decided not to fight the inevitable."

"Sadly, money ruined lives," Beth said.

"Look at the bright side. It brought us together. If we hadn't dived into the world of Nancy Drew and Bess, who knows what might have happened."

Ethan went behind the counter and set the bag down. "Not bad for your first and last case."

Beth said, "It was fun, even if it was a little scary."

I gave her a wink. "We could come out of retirement if necessary."

To keep reading, order your copy of Buttons & Burglary today!

Buttons & Burglary
A Craft and Ghost Cozy Mystery
Order Now

A FREE STORY FOR YOU

Have you enjoyed Ghosts & Gowns? Not ready to stop reading yet? If you sign up for my newsletter at www.lucin darace.com/newsletter, you will receive Cookies & Capers, which is the start of Lily and Milo's adventure in the Book-store Cozy Mystery Series, as my thank-you gift for choosing to receive my newsletter.

Cookies & Capers

I stood in front of the old wood and glass door as I pocketed the keys to the Cozy Nook Bookshop. Aunt Mimi had signed her bookstore over to me. She said it felt like giving me her baby. But I loved the shop as much as my aunt did. We had worked together for the last twelve years. After attending the University of Maine, I had a degree in history and education. I had always wanted to be a teacher, but jobs were scarce and after substituting for a few years, I moved back to my hometown of Pembroke, Maine, and Aunt Mimi hired me as soon as I unpacked my suitcase.

Spending time with my aunt, learning the business, had been the best experience. I offered to buy the shop when she wanted to retire, but she wouldn't hear of it. As long as she had free books for life, and her long-term boyfriend Nate, she said it was a fair deal. From my point of view, I had built-in backup for years to come.

Now that I was the bookshop owner, Aunt Mimi was no longer coming in every day which meant her cat, Phoenix, wasn't either and the space felt empty without a kitty lying in the window or skulking about as kitties do. I was off to the Pembroke Animal Palace to see if I could find a match.

It was a short walk in the bright noonday sun. The spring air from the ocean carried a tang of salt, but the breeze was refreshing. I waved to one of my best friends, Gage Erikson, as he drove past in his police-issued sedan. My heart fluttered in my chest.

He was a detective on the force. Not that we had much crime in our small seaside town. But one of these days I was going to get brave and tell him I had been carrying a torch for him since we were in ninth grade. What's the worst thing that could happen? We'd still be best friends, right?

I continued down the brick sidewalk, waving to William North from the Sweet Spot Bakery. He was sweeping the area around the small bistro tables in front of the bakery. William was wearing a large pristine white apron and a wide smile. A deep inhale confirmed my suspicion. He was baking cookies. My mouth watered. I did a half turn and went back to where he was finishing up. "Good morning, William." I bobbed my head in the shop's direction. "What is that tantalizing smell?"

He held open the brightly polished glass door. "One of your favorites, Lily. Chocolate chip and pecan cookies. Can I interest you in one before you continue on your mission?"

I gave him a side-look. "Mission?"

He chuckled. "Over the years my Lulu had said you had two speeds, strolling and purposeful. Just now it was purposeful so hence you're on a mission."

"I'm going to the shelter, hoping to find a kitty. The shop

is lonely now that Phoenix is home every day with Aunt Mimi, and I think a cat napping in the window adds an air of serenity to the place."

"Unless you're allergic."

He had a point, but I was not willing to be deterred. I smiled. "I'm always happy to deliver to a customer." I leaned over the glass bakery case, like a kid pressing her nose against the candy case. "You made sugar cookies too and frosted them?" I sighed. I was going to need to exercise more if he continued to bake all my favorites. He was smiling at me as I looked up. "Are the chocolate pecan ready?"

He wiggled his eyebrows. "I have a tray cooling in the back."

"Then can I have one of those and a sugar cookie, but to go?"

With a flick of his wrist, he snapped open a white bakery bag and called over his shoulder. "Jerilyn, would you please bring out the last batch of cookies?"

I heard a muffled, coming, and smiled. "It's good that Jerilyn stayed on." I said nothing about his beloved wife Lulu. Rumor had it she was ill and not doing well.

He nodded. "It is. She's a hard worker and excellent with the customers."

Jerilyn bustled in from the back room carrying a large stainless-steel tray. It was lined with parchment paper and cookies the size of the palm of my hand. It was going to taste so good with a hot cup of tea later.

William put two in the bag, along with two sugar cookies, and then he handed it to me. I paid for my cookies and thanked him. "Stop by the shop later. You might just get to meet my new fur baby."

"Sounds like a plan." He grinned and crossed his arms over his rounded midsection. "You're more like your aunt than you realize. Ever since she opened that bookshop, she's had a cat, too."

I paused, tucked the bakery bag in my tote, and with my hand on the door, I turned and gave him a wide grin. "And now it's time I carry on the tradition." With a jaunty wave, I called, "Wish me luck."

Cookies & Capers is only available by signing up for my newsletter – sign up for it here at www.lucindarace.com/newsletter

LOVE TO READ?

**All ebooks, paperback and audio copies can be ordered
from my website at:
Shop at Lucinda Race**

Cozy Mystery Books
A Bookstore Cozy Mystery Series
Books & Bribes
*It was an ordinary day until the book of Practical Magic conked Lily
on the head causing her to see stars. And then she discovered her
cat, Milo, could talk.*

Catnaps & Crimes
*The fun continues as Lily practices her magic and needs to
investigate another murder.*

Tea & Trouble
*A fall festival, reading tea leaves and a few clues propel Lily into a
new murder investigation.*

Scares & Dares

Ghost and Gowns June 2025
Buttons & Burglary July 2025
Ribbons & Robbery August 2025

Witches of Robins Pointe
A Paranormal Cozy Mystery Series
Inherited Magic & Murder January 2026
Touch of Magic February 2026
Waiting for Magic March 2026

Cowboys of River Junction
Second Chances in Montana
Twenty years later, Renee and Hank are back where they fell in love, but reality is like a spring frost, and is a long-distance relationship their only option for their second chance?

Stars Over Montana
The cowboy broke her heart, but he never stopped loving her. Now, she's back ready to run her grandfather's ranch…

Hiding in Montana
Can love flourish while danger lurks in the shadows?

Moonlight Over Montana
From the smoldering ash, she realizes he's all the family she and her daughter need.
rm can lead to love.

Price Family Romance Series
Breathe
Her dream come true may be the end of his…
Crush
The first time they met was fleeting; the second time restarted her heart.
<u>Blush</u>

Arielle Clark is a famous artist with a painful past. When her first love comes to town, ghosts from the past are resurrected. But can the embers of love still linger after all these years?

Standalone Titles

Shamrocks are a Girl's Best Friend

Will a bit of Irish luck and a matchmaking uncle give Kelly and Tric a chance to find love?

The Matchmaker and The Marine

She vowed never to love again. His career in the Marines crushed his ability to love. Can undeniable chemistry and a leap of faith overcome their past?

<u>Sundaes on Sunday</u>

A widowed school teacher and the airline pilot whose little girl is determined to bring her daddy and the lady from the ice cream shop together for a second chance at love.

Barrett

Has the last man standing finally met his match?

Marie

Career-focused city girl discovers small town chances

Holiday Heart Wishes

Heartfelt wishes and holiday kisses…

<u>Holiday Heart Wishes</u>

Hockey, holidays, and a slap shot to the heart.

<u>Christmas in July</u>

She's the hometown girl with the hometown advantage. Right?

<u>A Secret Santa Christmas</u>

Christmas just isn't Holly's thing, but will a family secret help her find the true meaning of Christmas?

SOCIAL MEDIA

Follow Me on Social Media

Like my Facebook page
Join Lucinda's Heart Racer's Reader Group on Facebook
Twitter @lucindarace
Instagram @lucindaraceauthor
BookBub
Goodreads
Pinterest
YouTube

ABOUT THE AUTHOR

AAward-winning and best-selling author Lucinda Race is a lifelong fan of fiction who fell in love with cozy mysteries and romance novels as a young girl. While her childhood friends dreamed of becoming doctors and engineers, Lucinda was already dreaming of crafting captivating novels filled with heart, hope, and happily ever afters.

Though her writing journey began with nonfiction, her passion for storytelling never wavered. She returned to her true calling—creating the beloved McKenna Family Romance series and the Paranormal Cozy Nook Bookstore Series— writing the kinds of stories she loves to read. Whether she's weaving a heartwarming romance or a paranormal cozy mystery, her fingers practically fly across the keyboard.

Lucinda lives in the rolling hills of western Massachusetts with her two little dogs—a miniature long-haired dachshund and a shih tzu mix rescue—who are always by her side. When she's not immersed in writing mystery, suspense, or romance, she's curled up with a book, devouring everything she can get her hands on.

www.ingramcontent.com/pod-product-compliance
Lightning Source LLC
Chambersburg PA
CBHW060410310726
48976CB00003B/997